Abbey

Gary R. Hope

"Abbey" by Gary R. Hope. ISBN 978-1-62137-831-0 (softcover).

Published 2016 by Virtualbookworm.com Publishing Inc., P.O. Box 9949, College Station, TX, 77842, US.

Previous books by Gary R. Hope:

NON-FICTION

Got Truth?

Gary's Hope

Scéal

The White Book

FICTION

It's Too Late To Die Young Now

This book is dedicated to "LOVE"

The love of the Lord,

The love of your family, and

The love of that special someone who makes your eyes sparkle every time you see them.

Table of Contents

Chapter 1

THE $2,500 ABHINANDAN just made for less than five minutes of simple computer work was filling his mind with all sorts of thoughts. He could pay off most of his remaining debt from the doctoral program at Virginia Tech. He could put a down payment on a nice, reliable car. Or, he could purchase a new hand-tailored suit he'd been dreaming of. Abbey, as his friends called him, was only a few weeks away from completing his PhD in Computational Science and Engineering and was negotiating with several companies over job opportunities. He needed a reliable car to get him to the various interviews, but he wanted a new hand-tailored suit. He also knew that his starting salary would enable him to pay off the last of his student debts rather easily. So, the decision boiled down to a new car or a new suit. Some women are impressed with cars, but all women are impressed by a man in an expensive suit. It was an easy decision for him.

He had just been paid for doing a little side job for someone that required him to hack into the computer system of an investment firm. He was assured this simple job was not to steal anything, not to jeopardize any accounts, nor to do anything illegal. His contact only wanted some information because he was curious. One of his greatest strengths, aside from his computer genius, was being able to read people. He could sense this man was telling him the truth, that he only wanted the information for his own personal knowledge. And, the fact that the job was so simple and quick made it an easy decision for him.

Abbey was a much sought after commodity from many high tech companies and from the federal government. During his first year in the doctoral program he made a name for himself nationally when he devised a program and engineered the software that enabled computers to significantly increase their capabilities. And, even more incredibly, to enable these computers to "think" for themselves, without needing input or data from outside (outside, meaning human help). What he had designed and perfected was beyond cutting edge. He not only pushed the limits of computational science where no one had ever been. He was operating in areas where others couldn't even comprehend.

The Defense Department and the CIA were both heavily recruiting him, as were several major technology companies nationwide—especially those in Silicon Valley, California. Unfortunately for the government, they couldn't compete with the salary scales of these billion dollar companies, all of whom wanted this computer wizard on their payrolls. He knew he was going to hit it rich very soon and he was in no hurry to choose. He had enjoyed his tenure at Virginia Tech and had become a Hokie through and through. But, the winters in the highlands of Virginia, fighting the wind and cold were not on his short list of job locations. However, unbeknownst to the firms in California, moving to the land of fruits and nuts was not very high on his priority list either. He was simply using them in his negotiations with other companies to drive his salary requirements higher.

He grew up in the mountains of North Carolina, in the little town of Boone, where his father and mother were both professors at Appalachian State University. His parents immigrated to the U.S. as college students from a village in India, high up in the Himalayas, called Jabalpur. Abbey had been born in the U.S. and was as Americanized as he could be—much to his parent's chagrin. Although he could understand a little of his parent's native dialects, his normal speech was 100% American, with just a hint of southern twang, for effect. Aside from his computational genius, the other quality that set him apart from his peers was his movie star good looks. The perfect posture on his 6'1" frame, which was accentuated by wavy, black hair (maybe just a tad too long), perfectly straight, white teeth and the facial features that made college girls swoon and all other women dream lusty thoughts of forbidden interludes.

One of his two weaknesses, if they can be called that, is a distinct and overwhelming rapaciousness for a pretty woman—especially a shapely, pretty blonde. He had a great appreciation for the beauty of women, but he had a weakness and an infatuation for a beautiful blonde. And, apparently, most of the attractive blondes in Blacksburg had, at one time or another, been on the arm of Abbey. He was not a one-woman man. This greatly concerned his parents, who were still a little old-fashioned and tried as hard as they could to convince him, to coerce him, to blackmail him and to bribe him into marrying someone of Indian descent. It didn't work.

He loved his parents and respected them in nearly everything, except his personal life. They were stuck in the past a little too much for him. Their lifestyles and customs of old India were simply not what he had become, or wanted for himself. He listened to them, out of respect, but he did what he wanted to

3

do. Not what custom required or expected him to do. He never lived in India and the caste system and religions there were foreign to him. He visited a few times, but never enjoyed it— except for the time he spent with his grandfather—who still lived there. His grandfather was the one person he listened to— and he listened to him in every aspect of his life.

His grandfather, Ramesh, has lived in India his entire life and knew the famous Maharishi Mahesh Yogi very well. In fact, they went to the same schools and learned religious beliefs and creeds from the same teachers. They were close friends during their childhoods and school years, but it quickly became apparent to Abbey's grandfather (as a young man), that Transcendental Meditation and the "state of enlightenment" was fool's gold. He broke away from Maharishi Yogi and his cults, before they became famous by luring celebrities and rock stars to the foothills of the Himalayas, with the promises of "inner calmness" and "spiritual peace" from across the universe.

The Maharishi tried to convince his friend to return to the fold and help him once his followers started multiplying. But Ramesh had found his own inner peace and had discovered all the answers he ever needed to know, in Jesus Christ. He was ostracized, ridiculed and outcast for his Christian beliefs, but he knew the truth when he saw it and refused to be bullied and threatened because of his beliefs. He was a great influence on Abbey as a youth and young man, for his courage and for his faith—which Abbey is still experimenting with.

Ramesh was greatly distressed when the Maharishi's public persona took a hit after the Beatles affair, when it was rumored that the master was a little more interested in Mia Farrow's sister than he was in all things eternal. Then he really became disenchanted when it seemed as though the Maharishi was more interested in making money than in saving souls. When the teacher died in 2008, his U.S. assets alone were over $300 million. Ramesh was sad his friend had died, and he was also sad to learn of the houses, cars and money he had accumulated in the name of spirituality.

His grandfather lives alone now in the same small village where he grew up. His wife died a few years ago and he now devotes all his time to teaching the Gospel and converting souls. Abbey misses seeing his grandfather and cherishes the memory of his grandmother.

Chapter 2

SILICON VALLEY COMPANIES WERE NOW FIGHTING over the rights to hire Abbey. His reputation was growing more and more lucrative with each passing week. His knowledge and expertise could mean millions of dollars in innovations for the company lucky enough to get him. He was aware of this. He also knew he would be going nowhere near California (except for vacation), but they didn't need to know that—not just yet. He had been negotiating with several east coast companies, mostly in the New York metropolitan area, and a few new companies from North Carolina. This is what intrigued him—North Carolina companies.

It seems as though Winston-Salem, North Carolina has cultivated and stimulated a technology growth sector that is expanding, not only in numbers and capital, but also in reputation and stature. This new growth appeals to him. Unlimited opportunities are what he's looking for. That, and he gets to stay in North Carolina—if they can match what Silicon Valley is offering. There are two companies in Winston-Salem that are especially aggressive in pursuing him: Simplexicon Technologies and Lonewolf Enterprises. The Silicon Valley companies had already made offers and he knew what his market worth was—or should be. The question was if these North Carolina companies had the capital and courage to match (or come close), to the offers already on the table. He knew if they could, he'd stay in North Carolina.

He was offered $225,000 a year by several California companies. That number disappointed him a little, but he reasoned it was simply a "starting" salary. He knew he'd quickly advance. After all, when it came to computers and computational science, Abbey was playing chess, while everyone else was playing checkers.

He went on second and third interviews with Simplexicon and Lonewolf and each was prepared to make him an offer. His next visit was the day of reckoning, the day that would decide whether he would live in California, New York or North Carolina. Simplexicon offered him a company car, a membership to Gold's Gym, a membership to Maple Chase Country Club and $250,000 a year to start—with the provision of adjusting that salary after six months. He was stunned. He was prepared to accept around $200,000 in order to stay in North Carolina. He almost accepted the offer on the spot. Almost. He was overwhelmed with the offer, but he still hadn't talked to Lonewolf Enterprises. Although he didn't think they could, or would, match this very generous offer, his analytical mind told him to at least check it out. So he did.

Lonewolf was a recent startup company that was backed financially by Wake Forest Baptist Hospital and Forsyth Medical Hospital. It specialized in cutting edge technologies in the health care system that enabled doctors and scientists to push as far and as fast as they could into the cures of cancers and heart diseases. They needed computers and systems that were dynamic and beyond the realm of imagination to look for innovative ways to fight and cure these diseases. They needed Abbey more than he needed them. In final negotiations, he finally realized this.

On his final interview, instead of offering him a salary, the president of the company asked him what it would take to get him to sign with Lonewolf. He had rehearsed this scenario overnight and quickly and emphatically said he would need $407,125. The president never blinked. Instead, he looked back at him for about thirty seconds with no reply, then said, "How about $250,000?" Now it was Abbey's turn not to blink, which was hard for him to do since his heart was racing at about two hundred beats a minute. He waited another sixty seconds, never taking his gaze off the eyes of the president, and said, "$337,850." The president wasted no time now and replied, "My final offer is $275,000....take it or leave it."

One of Abbey's greatest abilities, aside from his genius with computers, is his ability to read people—unerringly and accurately. He now had to trust his instincts implicitly. He looked back at the president and held his gaze until the president finally looked down at his desk. That gave Abbey all the information he needed; he said "If you want me, my final offer is $314,150." The president called his secretary and told her to bring in Abbey's contract. He took the document and wrote in $314,150. They shook hands and they both smiled. They were each very happy with the results.

Abbey and his grandfather kept a daily email communication between them for years. He could not start his day without reading the few lines his grandfather had left him overnight. Sometimes it was only a sentence or two, sometimes only a word or two. Always, it was insightful and helpful to his grandson. He felt there were days when his grandfather could sense his concerns and anxiousness. Somehow, the daily email from his grandfather directly addressed his issues and thoughts—he never understood how this happened. How did his grandfather know what he was thinking and what he needed from 12,000 miles away? It was a mystery he didn't understand, nor did he want to understand—he just didn't want to lose it.

The night he accepted the job in Winston-Salem he emailed his grandfather with the great news. After his parents, he wanted him to be the next to know that his future was now a reality that he could plan on. With all the excitement of the day, it was hard for him to sleep that night. Almost as much as the excitement of the new job, was the anticipation of what his grandfather would say to him. He couldn't wait till the sun came up in the morning. He started checking his emails about 4:30 AM. Soon, the message from his grandfather came through. As usual, it was short and insightful:

"A SINGLE DREAM IS MORE POWERFUL THAN A THOUSAND REALITIES."

He had a few loose ends to tie up in Blacksburg and at Virginia Tech before he started his new job with Lonewolf Technologies. He drove back up there and gave all his friends the news. Some were happy for him, some were happy for themselves because he was leaving. With Abbey out of the way, maybe they could be the stars now, maybe they could get some attention. Jealousy can often bring out the worst in people and expose characteristics and truths that were hidden for months and years—even in those you thought were your friends. He was popular and had rock star status in the technology underground in and around the academic circles of Virginia. Everyone came to him for advice, including his teachers and mentors. A person with Abbey's abilities came along very seldom.

He had a few days to disassemble his array of personal computer and programming equipment for the trip to his new home in Winston-Salem, but first, he had a few parting gifts he wanted to make. This weekend the UNC Tarheel basketball team was in town to play his beloved Hokies. In years past, Virginia Tech had a fighting chance against Carolina and won some of the games (not many, but some). Now, however, they had no chance. Football ruled at Tech and basketball was simply something to observe until spring football practice started. This irked him. He hated to lose, especially to the baby blue Heels.

He knew there was nothing that could change the outcome of the game, Carolina was just too good for Tech, they had too many good players. And even though there was nothing he could do to change this fact, maybe there was something he could do to make the game a little closer. He went back to his little dump of an apartment and opened up his array of computer equipment—much of which he built himself, while waiting on patents from the government. He knew all visiting teams stayed at the best hotel in town, the Golden Arms Inn. It was child's play for him to hack into the hotel's mainframe and set up his plan.

Tomorrow's game was televised, as all UNC games are, with a noon start. Which meant the coaches would ensure all the players got to their rooms early and were in bed at least by 11:00 PM. He found the alarm system for the hotel and programmed a test for the fire alarm network and sprinkler system at 3:00 AM. The fire alarm itself would probably have been enough to disrupt the sleep of the UNC players, having to get out of bed and go outside at 3:00 AM. Maybe they could've gone back to sleep after that—maybe not. But he knew if the sprinklers were also activated and everyone got thoroughly soaked, it would really make it difficult to get a good night's rest.

It all worked. The fire alarm went off and the sprinklers soaked everyone on the team's floor, but not any of the other guests floors. And UNC only won the game by 9 points (the spread was 19). The game's commentators noticed a lack of energy from the UNC players and commented on their "tired legs." He knew his prank would never affect the outcome of the game—the Tarheels were simply too good. But, in the end, it did make him feel a whole lot better for his team to win a "moral victory" by holding the score to less than 10 points.

Chapter 3

BEFORE HE LEFT HE HAD TO SAY HIS GOODBYE'S to a few old girlfriends as well. He was special to them all. Abbey saw each of these women as they truly were—glorious, radiant and spectacular. Imperfect, because he was not limited by his eyesight, he looked at women by seeing beyond what was visible to the eye. Women reacted to him because they sensed he searched out the beauty that was in them. That feeling overwhelmed everything else, and they couldn't avoid their desire to release that beauty and envelop him in it.

 He assured each one they were special to him and that he would never forget them. He told them what they wanted to hear, what they needed to hear. He told them the truth. Though he was never serious with any of these young ladies, they were all memorable to him, as he was to them. He treated them like no man ever had before. He treated them like they were the most important woman on earth to him. And for that night— they were. He loved women. He loved their scent, he loved the softness of their skin and the color of their eyes. He loved the way a woman's underclothing barely touches her skin. How it rides on a cushion of air, brushing her skin like an angel's wings. He made them each think they were his princess for the night. He had that effect.

But, he also knew he wouldn't have time to be making the four hour drive from Winston-Salem up to Blacksburg for a girl. No. There would be plenty of other women in his new home— he was sure of that. He had driven around Winston-Salem during his interviews and toured the campus at Wake Forest University, which seemed to attract all the rich, beautiful, upwardly mobile young socialites that didn't score high enough on their SAT's, or were too pretty to get in Duke. He liked what he saw.

He also discovered there was a predominantly women's college in town. Salem College was small, but from what he could see, it was located in a very attractive older section of the city. They prided themselves on their "historical" buildings, some of which were nearly three hundred years old. He found this odd, since his heritage was from India, where the barber shops there were usually three hundred years old. And "old" in India was measured in terms of centuries—not years. But he liked Salem College. There was something about it. He was sure he'd be back.

He closed all his accounts, said his goodbye's at the school and had nothing left to do but pack up his computer equipment and his personal belongings from the apartment. He glanced at the newspaper as he was packing and noticed that the University of Virginia (Tech's arch rival) was traveling later that night to Greenville, N.C., for the first time ever, to play East Carolina University in a baseball game the next day. He kept staring at the paper, but he wasn't reading it. He was thinking.

Before he packed up his computers, he found his way into the GPS navigational system the University of Virginia was using. Since this game with East Carolina would be the first game ever played between the two schools, he was pretty sure they didn't know how to actually get to Greenville, N.C. without using the GPS. His plan was ingenious and simple. All he had to do was substitute one letter and let the nature of things carry forth. He went into the GPS and changed the "N" into a "S." The bus driver would now be routed to Greenville, S.C. —-not Greenville, N.C.

The next morning he read the email from his grandfather, which was the first thing he did every morning. It read,

"IT'S NOT WHAT YOU DO, BUT HOW MUCH LOVE YOU PUT INTO IT THAT MATTERS."

Although he had done very little—he loved his little prank. He heard on the news that the proposed baseball game between Virginia and East Carolina had been postponed due to "travel problems." He smiled as he pulled out of Blacksburg and headed to his new home in the rolling hills of Winston-Salem, North Carolina.

He spent the first night in Winston-Salem at the Marriot, downtown. He had an appointment the next morning with a real estate agent to show him some properties. However, he really didn't need any help. He already knew where he wanted to live—the Nissen Building. He had checked on-line and determined the condos at the Nissen had what he was looking for. A downtown location, a bar, a swimming pool, a small gym, dry-cleaning pick- up and delivery service, grocery delivery service, hardwood floors, a fireplace, and a fantastic panoramic view of the city and mountains.

His mind was made up. He didn't even want to see other places—-this is where he would live. He excitedly emailed his grandfather with his choice of home and his feelings about starting his new job the next day. He had great confidence in himself, but expressed a little apprehension to his grandfather about whether he could do all Lonewolf Technologies was expecting him to do. Again, he found it hard to sleep that night, and awoke early to read the email his grandfather had written back,

"WHETHER YOU THINK YOU CAN OR CAN'T, YOU'RE RIGHT."

He could. His first morning at Lonewolf Technology was spent meeting all the various department heads and staff. Everyone gave him their "wish list" for things they wanted him to help them with. He wondered why they didn't have some lowly paid programmer to do all this simple work. He was beginning to think he underestimated the direction Lonewolf wanted to go. Then, the excitement started. A meeting was set for two o'clock whereby the various heads of medical departments from Baptist Hospital and Forsyth Hospital all had the opportunity to meet him. This is why he was hired, to make their dreams come true. To put into reality what their imaginations could only think of. To take them here, there, everywhere.

They needed his expertise to help them formulate ideas, program test results, take all their incoming data and extrapolate all this information into something useful. They needed Abbey and his computers to take all their hard work and ideas and THINK for them—to take them where they didn't know where to go—but needed to go. He was excited and couldn't wait to start.

After work, he met the realtor and toured the condo at the Nissen building. He decided immediately it was what he wanted and signed the contract before he left. He was now the owner of a two bedroom, beautiful, unfurnished condo. Back to the Hyatt for one more night. He shopped on- line for furniture and chose what he wanted from a company that could deliver the next day. He didn't choose exactly what he wanted, but he chose what they had in stock that could be delivered. No more hotel living for him. He wanted to get everything delivered and settled. The staff at the Nissen would direct the movers and make sure everything was set up—another of the amenities they offered. He was ready for his life to come together.

Chapter 4

HE WAS FINALLY AT HOME NOW, all his furniture had been delivered and he was set. It would take an extra day or two to complete the installation of his personal computers, which would take up the entire second bedroom. He was excited, tired and hungry. He hadn't been able to do any shopping so he decided to walk around downtown Winston and find something quick and easy. Before he left, he checked his computer and found another message from his grandfather,

"EVERYONE YOU KNOW IS FIGHTING A BATTLE YOU KNOW NOTHING ABOUT. BE KIND. ALWAYS."

He thought about this as he walked down Trade Street, which was the heart of the arts district in Winston-Salem. He was impressed with all the galleries and shops, but now he was hungry and wanted something quick and filling. He stepped in an Irish bar called "Finnegan's Wake" and instantly liked what he saw. A cute waitress came to his table and he ordered something tall, black and foamy while he looked over the menu. He must've looked a little confused because the owner of the bar stopped at his table and asked if he had any questions.

Opie, the owner, was a friendly guy and a few years older than him. But he had a way about him that made Abbey instantly like him. Opie recommended the Blarney Burger, with cheese and bacon and a side order of sweet potato fries. Abbey agreed. Opie wanted to know all about Abbey and his new job, where he lived, if he had a girlfriend and any other information he could get. The two seemed to naturally hit it off with each other and were enjoying their conversation when the bar manager came over and whispered something to Opie, which instantly changed his mood. Opie shook his head and cursed under his breath. Abbey asked him if everything was okay. The bar manager had just informed Opie that the beer supplier they had been using was raising his rates again. The third increase in the last eight months.

Abbey was a good listener, so while he waited for the Blarney Burger, Opie told him all about it. This beer distributor had seemed nice and friendly when Finnegan's Wake opened and offered Opie a great deal if he would only sign a contract with him for five years. The distributor seemed like a great guy and was very friendly. Opie trusted him and didn't read the fine print. The great deal lasted four months, then he increased his rates. Then four months later he increased them again. Now, another increase. Opie was being gouged and because of his contract, there was little he could do about it. Abbey asked the name of the distributor and Opie spat the name out (amidst some colorful North Carolina slang words). Abbey would look into this. First, he wanted to dig into the burger and fries and sneak a peek at a table of Wake Forest coeds nearby—one of whom happened to be blonde and very pretty.

He enjoyed his dinner at Finnegan's Wake. He'd found a comfortable place to visit and a good guy to talk with in Opie. He didn't really enjoy being around a lot of people. But he liked the companionship of his new friend and the table full of young coeds only enhanced the atmosphere. Abbey treasured his aloneness—but not loneliness. He liked solitude—not society— except when that society involved the presence of a pretty young lady. Especially a pretty, blonde young lady.

Before he went to sleep that night, he sat out on his balcony and enjoyed the silence of late night. The hum of crickets and the symphony of the cicadas (or were they locusts)? The occasional hooting of the night owl—calling for a late dinner. Calling for all mice and rodents and little bunnies to run from one bush to another in the vain attempt of trying to escape his attention. He liked the sounds of nature in his city home. He also liked Opie and decided to look into Full Moon Beer Distributors—covertly, that is, and see what was going on with all those rate increases.

Back at work, he expressed his concerns to his boss (the President) about all the "requests" he'd been getting from everyone to do all sorts of menial, inconsequential computer jobs. The sort of stuff any geek or hack could handle. He was not just any sort of geek. The President knew this and sent out a memo to all personnel that Abbey was not part of the IT department and no employee was to request anything from him. He gave them all the word: Abbey took his directions only from the President. His direction being to do whatever your imagination will allow you to do. Go beyond the known and into the unknown, go to the back of beyond. He had no set hours, no agenda and virtually no one to answer to. They wanted no restrictions on his mind and imagination. He did not disappoint them.

After work, he walked down 4th St., investigating all the various bars and restaurants, doing a lot of window shopping and admiring the local female population. He discovered Winston- Salem was indeed a scenic area. He just couldn't get out of his mind about the beer distributor that was gouging his new friend Opie on his rates. As he passed by Skippy's Hot Dogs and a wine bar named Corks, Caps and Taps, he decided he would investigate. Only to take a look into Full Moon's website and whatever else he could get into—which meant everything. He wanted to see exactly what was going on here.

Later that night, back in is his condo he wrote his grandfather and gave him a short version of what was happening to his new friend and mentioned he "might" try to help, if he could. Usually, his grandfather would reply to all his emails within a few hours. This time, he immediately responded with this reply:

"ALL THAT IS NECESSARY FOR EVIL TO SUCCEED IS THAT GOOD MEN DO NOTHING."

Abbey was a good man...and he would definitely not do nothing.

Before he went to bed he went out to his balcony to sit for a few minutes in the solitude of the night. This was a special time for him, his time. No work demands, no timetables, no pressures—just time for him to think about things—or not. Most times he simply liked the silence; unbroken by the sounds of the night, or even by a thought.

After a suitable time of reflection, his mind started thinking again of women. Of blonde women he had known before, of women he wanted to know again, of women he hoped to know in the near future. And, of all things spiritual. He was unclear where he was headed on his own spiritual path. His parents have their own plan, his grandfather has his ideas—which he respects. But he was still processing, asking questions, thinking. He wrote another email to his grandfather asking him about his spiritual journey, hoping for some insight and some direction. A minute or two after he hit the send button, he again received a quick reply from his grandfather.

He was anxious to read what his grandfather would say about his spiritual journey and where it had taken him. This is the message he received,

"I AM NOT, NOR ARE YOU, NOR IS ANY HUMAN ON A SPIRITUAL JOURNEY. YOUR SPIRIT, ABHINANDAN, IS ON A HUMAN JOURNEY."

Chapter 5

FULL MOON BEER DISTRIBUTORS had a very informative and professional website. He was impressed with the information and the ease one could navigate through the pages. He was also impressed with the mission statement and the page detailing all the public service good works and donations Full Moon was doing in the community. He just didn't believe any of it. The classic example of something apparently being too good to be true.

He didn't really care about all the fluff and corporate mumbo jumbo. He was more interested in the President of Full Moon— the man who signed the initial contract with Opie at Finnegan's Wake. The website said Lamar Fletcher started Full Moon about 14 years ago and had grown it and increased its revenues substantially. He remained President and Chairman of the Board, his wife was Vice-President and his brother was the Chief Financial Officer. Wasn't that all nice and tidy? Maybe a little too much so—at least that's what Abbey thought.

Since Full Moon wasn't a public company, their financial records weren't public information. So Abbey had to do a little "undercover" work. It was simple enough to hack into their website and see their revenues for the last fiscal year. And also to see what Full Moon was charging each customer for their services and products. As he suspected, there was a wide range of rates for essentially the same service and the same product.

For a large chain restaurant, Full Moon would charge a medium rate for a keg of beer to be delivered. However, for a small pub like Finnegan's, or a few others around town, Full Moon was charging about 25% more. Finnegan's had initially paid the same rate as the large chains, but three increases later had led to the 25% increase. This bothered him. He could not find any other financial information that would help him understand anything. He had to dig deeper. The IRS is a huge, gargantuan institution. But their data base was only protected by a simple fire wall, and not even the top-of-the-line security networks. Abbey was disappointed in our government's lackadaisical and sophomoric attempts to stop breaches in its security.

It took him about fifteen minutes to get into the IRS files and find the W-2 statements for Lamar Fletcher and his wife. Our good old boy Lamar had a net income last year of $1.3 million, and his wife made $750,000. He didn't really know if this was appropriate or not—it seemed very high to him. What interested him most was that Lamar's, and his wife's, salaries had increased nearly 35% in each of the last four years while sales had only increased about 7% each year. It seemed perfectly clear to him that the owners were lining their pocketbooks with the increases from companies like Finnegan's Wake and other small businesses who had signed on with Full Moon.

He then checked the city/county tax registers to reinforce what he already knew—the Fletcher's were living the good life. They weren't doing anything illegal, but in his opinion, they were doing something immoral—which to him was worse. Two years ago they purchased a $1,125,000 home in Bent Tree

Estates. They have no children, but they have four cars: two new Mercedes, a three year old Hummer and a year old Corvette. Plus, they owned his and her matching Indian motorcycles. The Fletchers travelled in style. She was a member of the Junior League and he was an officer in the Masons. They were both very prominent and influential (through large donations) in the United Way—especially the Food Bank and Red Cross. They had spent a lot of time building their reputations. It was important for them to be noticed and respected.

As far as he could tell, they paid their taxes. They didn't do anything that could get them in trouble with the government or the law, and everything seemed normal—too normal. On the company's website were links to "Contact Us", which led to sales, marketing, delivery, employment and other departmental websites. It also had a link for sending a message to the President. This is what he needed. From that link, he could follow it to the President's other websites and email addresses—his personal ones. For most computer techs, there are no secrets in the world. Anything people email or text; any websites they delve into; anything they THINK they're doing in the privacy of their homes is actually totally transparent to people who understand how technology and computers work— like Abbey.

He had never delved into people's personal accounts before. The only exceptions were when he would secretly check the emails from a girl he was dating to see what she was telling her friends about him. But, that was the game of love—and anything is fair in love. It didn't take long to find a website that both Lamar and his wife were visiting often—several times each week: "Sharing and Caring."

This website was also protected by a minimal firewall, that tried to keep out the casual hacker. It was no match for someone of his abilities. It was protected not because it was illegal, but because it was not the type of site you'd want your mama to find out about. "Sharing and Caring" was a site that helped couples set up threesomes, foursomes and group sex in the Piedmont Triad metropolitan area. The site listed all the possibilities and had pictures of willing participants (including the Fletchers). Members could log in and peruse pictures of other couples and find who did what and who wanted to do this or that—it was very specific.

What people did in their personal lives did not matter at all to him. But gouging your customers, and his friend, in order to live the high life and walk on the wild side did matter to him. He had to think about this. He had to find a way to use this information, anonymously, to help those who couldn't help themselves.

Abbey enjoyed walking the downtown area of Winston. He found a local pub at the far end of 4th Street called Foothills Brewery that he enjoyed visiting. He enjoyed it because they had a local beer called "Liquid Sunshine" and another named "A Taste of Honey" that he liked. He was really a wine drinker, but he did enjoy a beer, especially when it was delivered to his table by the night manager of the bar. Anne, the manager, greeted him and welcomed him to Foothills and recommended the Cuban sandwich for his first meal there. He didn't really care about the food , which turned out to be delicious. He was more interested in Anne: Was she married? Was she involved? Was she available?

However, Anne didn't wait tables. He had a younger tattooed girl doing that for him. She was nice, but a bit young and dark-haired for him. No, he was interested in Anne. But how could he talk to her? She was busy behind the counter and in the office. He kept hanging around, but Anne didn't come back near his table. After another glass of "Liquid Sunshine" he decided he'd take up the quest another night when he had more time—but, he would definitely be back. Anne was very interesting.

On his way back to the condo he stopped to window shop at an art gallery. There was a small, framed print hanging in the window that read, "Winston-Salem's calling me, and I must go." He thought of sending it to his grandfather. As he was smiling over the print, he noticed a lady inside the store who was very attractive and who was looking back at him through the window. This is where his sense of confidence was better than most. Whereas most men might shy away, or at least look away, or look down at their hands when a pretty woman caught their gaze. He did not. He looked directly back at her and didn't move or blink until she finally did. He loved this little game—and he never lost.

She finally went behind the counter when a customer inside wanted to buy something, but kept glancing back out the window at him. He pretended to be interested in another object on display, but he knew that she knew that he was only standing there because of her. He was thinking if he should enter the store and maybe buy something. But discretion and the art of romance and the allure of the chase told him to catch her glance one more time—smile, then walk away. Few women ever forgot the moment when Abbey smiled at them. He was confident she wouldn't forget either.

It was a good night for him. Anne at Foothill's and now the lady in the art shop—Winston-Salem was going to be a nice place indeed. As usual, he looked forward to getting back home and relaxing and reflecting on the day's events and reading the email from his grandfather. He had purchased a bundle of firewood from a local market and wanted to try out his fireplace. He liked sitting around a fire. Not for the warmth, but for symbolic reasons. For ceremony. For the dreams he held of evenings in his youth, and the memories of sitting around a fire with his grandfather. He opened the daily email from his grandfather once the fire started and read it on his tablet in front of the flames:

"GOD WANTS TO USE US. WE ARE NOT ALL CALLED TO DO THE SAME THING. BUT WE ARE CALLED TO DO SOMETHING. MAKE THAT SOMETHING GREAT."

Chapter 6

YEARS EARLIER, when his grandfather was explaining to him what Transcendental Meditation was, Abbey had hacked into their website just to check it out and see where all the money was actually going. He hadn't been on the website in a few years, but now he had a reason to use it for his personal use. He entered it quite easily and set up a fictitious account so he could send emails through this account, which would be impossible to ever trace back to him. He wanted to send an anonymous email to Lamar Fletcher, the President of Full Moon Distributors.

The email read, "Lamar, I know all about 'Sharing and Caring' and I don't care what you and your wife do with your private lives. However, I do care about the increased rates you're charging several customers in Winston-Salem. I urge you to reevaluate these rate increases and determine if it might be possible to only charge them what you're currently charging the rest of your customers. I'll give you a few days to think about this. In case you were wondering, it will be impossible for you (or anyone else) to trace this email. If the rates are lowered, you'll never hear from me again. If the rates are not lowered, everyone will hear from me again and your private affairs may not be so private any longer. This is the only warning you'll receive."

Two days later he stopped in Finnegan's to have another Blarney Burger, this time with a Diet Coke . He was watching his weight. Opie was smiling and slapping everyone on the back and telling corny jokes. "A skeleton came walking in my bar last night, looked at the bartender and said, give me a beer and a mop." Abbey laughed, even though he didn't want to, he laughed anyway. He liked the corny joke, but he liked seeing his friend's happiness even more.

He smiled at Opie and said, "You seem to be in a really good mood tonight my friend." Opie replied, "I am. We got great news in the mail today. Remember when I told you our rates had gone up considerably on our beer deliveries?" Abbey said, "Yes, I do remember you mentioning that."

"You'll never believe what happened. They lowered our rates back to what they were when we first started. It's incredible!"

"Wow" Abbey said, "What caused this?"

"I have no idea, and I don't really care. All I know is that now I can make payroll every week without having to worry myself to death. And by the way…that Blarney Burger is on the house!"

Even though Abbey was only drinking a Diet Coke, a warm sensation swept over him and gave him a buzz no alcohol could have ever done. He was looking forward to starting a fire in his fireplace later tonight and pouring himself a small glass of Riesling and contemplating the day's events, while possibly thinking a few blonde thoughts.

He had emailed his grandfather earlier that day and asked him how his health was. He was concerned and wanted to make sure his grandfather was doing well and taking care of himself. His grandfather always seemed to dismiss these concerns and always told him he was "Excellent!" Tonight's email was not much different. His grandfather wrote,

"GOOD HEALTH IS MERELY THE SLOWEST POSSIBLE RATE AT WHICH ONE CAN DIE."

The good news didn't last long. On his next visit to Foothill's Brewery he learned from a waiter that Anne was married. Disappointing to be sure, she was a lovely woman. Saturday would now be a shopping day, an art gallery shopping day. He was hoping there was a special on "blondes," especially the young lady he'd seen in the window. He was pretty sure he had charmed her with his smile the day he first saw her. He knew, from experience, women usually melted when he smiled at them.

He casually strolled up to the gallery window and again pretended to be window shopping , when in fact he was trying to fend off the glare from the sun to see if the blonde woman was in the store. He was squinting and couldn't seem to find an angle where he could see well, when someone tapped him on the shoulder.

"Can I help you find something?"

He turned to find the blonde woman he was searching for, holding a large bag and possessing the most alluring smile he'd ever seen. "I was just admiring that piece of artwork in the window." He said.

"Oh, you mean those paint cans up front there? We're doing a little remodeling and the painters left their supplies here while we closed for lunch."

It was not easy to embarrass Abbey. He was always poised, self-assured and composed. But her smile did something to him, and had caught him in an obviously awkward moment. His thoughts were momentarily jumbled and it took him a few moments before he could finally respond.

"No," he said, "not the paint cans at all. I was admiring your reflection in the window. It took my breath away." She stared at him for a moment, then smiled. And when she smiled at him, he nearly lost consciousness. He was incapable of any further comment at this moment. He knew no words that were relevant.

She finally said, "Would you like to share a pastry with me? I just got it fresh from Camino's down the street, it has an unusual flavor, not from around here, but irresistible to the taste." As he was trying to understand if she was really referring to the pastry, or him, she said "Sit down, I'll get us some coffee. Black?"

"No," he said, "I'm Indian. Really I'm American, but my family came from India."

"That's not what I meant." She replied, "Do you take your coffee black?" If he had been capable of blushing—he would have.

"Just some cream please." She went inside to get the coffee. He sat on the bench outside the shop and thought to himself "No one has ever done this to me, no one has ever made me fidget , made me fumble, made me …..what has she made me do"?

He was so lost in thought, he didn't notice her come back out the door holding two cups of coffee and struggling to open the door. He quickly jumped up to help and apologized—she smiled again—and again, he forgot what he was going to say.

"My name is Juliette, and you are?" It was as though she was speaking a foreign language. He truly didn't recognize a word she said. So, he just stared at her. "Are you okay?" she said. "Yes, I….what did you just say?" "I asked what your name is—do you remember it?"

"Yes, I'm sorry, it's Abhinandan, but my friends call me Abbey. And what is your name?" She smiled at his memory lapse again and said, "It's Juliette. Very nice to meet you Abhinandan." When she smiled at him, he didn't know whether to tie his shoes or play checkers. No quantitative, computational catechism had ever confounded him as much as her smile. He couldn't think. He couldn't talk. He couldn't act—he could barely remember his name.

After sitting in silence for a few moments and sipping his coffee, he remembered passing The Aperture Theater as he was walking down the street. He didn't notice what was playing— he didn't really care—he wasn't a movie person. But at that moment, his mind was totally void of any other thoughts. He couldn't think of anything else to say. His mind was racing as he thought to himself, "I don't understand why I can't think. This has never happened to me before. I have to say something or she'll think I've lost my mind."

He finally blurted out, "Would you like to go to the movie with me tonight?"

"What's playing?" she said.

"Umm, I think it's a foreign film that's supposed to be good."
(He actually had no idea what was playing)

She looked at him for a few seconds and said, "No, I'm sorry, I already have plans for tonight."

He felt as if the stock market had just crashed, as if his computer had contracted a horrible virus, and his dog had died—and he didn't even have a dog. As he tried to compose himself and think of a graceful way to continue the conversation, she turned to him, smiled and said, "But, I'll change my plans—I'd love to go."

Again, words seemed to elude his ability to employ them. She said, "Why don't you pick me up about 6:00 and we can have something to eat before the movie. I have to go back to work now, I'll see you tonight Abhinandan." And she went inside the store.

At least he thought she went inside the store. She could've just disappeared, or been abducted by aliens for all he knew. He was still incapable of comprehending what just happened to him. Finally, he did recover enough to rise from the bench and walk away….he just had no idea where he was walking to.

Chapter 7

IT WAS STILL SIX HOURS BEFORE HIS DATE and he was a combination of thrilled, excited, perplexed and confused. No woman had ever made him feel or act the way Juliette had, and he'd been with plenty of women. He needed some sort of release, some physical relaxation before tonight. He thought of tennis. He didn't actually play tennis—he just liked to hit balls. His father and mother both played and had always told him stories about the great Indian tennis pro Vijay Amritraj. Although he never saw Amritraj play tennis, since he was too young, he did see him act in the James Bond movie "Octopussy."

He wanted to emulate the great tennis pro, not on the courts, but for his character in the movie: suave, confident, handsome and a girl magnet. He also thought Vijay looked very cool in his tennis outfits. Abbey wanted to look like a tennis player, he just didn't want to sweat. He was entirely too cool for that. So, he dressed in his new Nike tennis outfit, gathered up his racket, cell phone, ipod , water bottle, towel and went to Hanes Park. There, he could find a remote clay court, rent a tennis ball machine which would send balls over the net to him and he wouldn't have to move—just stand there and hit them back.

He didn't really care if his shots went in the court or not. His main objective was to look good. Secondary goals were to get as much physical activity as he could without actually perspiring and to try and calm his nerves before he saw Juliette again tonight. Whereas hitting forehands and backhands had no perceivable effects on him, just thinking of Juliette made him break out in tiny beads of sweat. Who was this girl?

Juliette not only worked at the art gallery—she owned it. Her father bought if for her when she retired from the North Carolina Dance Theater. Juliette was from Marin County, California but had moved to Winston-Salem in the 10th grade to attend The University of North Carolina School of the Arts and study dance. She had graduated to become a leading ballerina in the NC Dance Theater—not the primary ballerina, but the next leading dancer. She was very dedicated and also very talented.

The life of a ballerina is short and hard. The physical demands that dancing requires from their bodies shortens their professional lives considerably. Juliette was no exception. Back problems, leg problems, feet issues—the whole gamut of injuries that beset ballerinas had taken their toll. After her third operation in two years, she decided she couldn't do it any longer. That's when her father bought her the art gallery. She loved Winston-Salem, had many friends and associates in the arts community and with the School of the Arts. Her parents wanted her to come back home to California where they were happily retired from his successful days as a hedge fund manager and were now living the life of leisure.

But Juliette didn't want to leave Winston-Salem. It suited her. She thought to herself, "I've got a feeling this is where I'm meant to be." The arts district was exciting. The people were friendly and all her friends were here, or in Charlotte—she wasn't leaving. So, her dad made the investment and Juliette was making a small profit from the gallery each month on her own. It did help that her mom sent her an allowance each month, however.

Juliette always had guys fawning over her. She was used to that type of behavior from men (and women). She had always been involved with either dancers or artists, never anyone like Abbey. Certainly no one with the casual gracefulness, confidence and appearance he possessed. She was used to men fumbling over words around her, but she wasn't used to the awkwardness she felt around him. He was different.

But Abbey didn't feel different. After stammering for words with Juliette and losing his composure around her, he felt like an awkward teenager. This had never happened to him before, even when he WAS a teenager. He was concerned. He needed to email his grandfather. He sent the email as soon as he got home from hitting tennis balls. He briefly told his grandfather about the experience and all the things that had gone wrong that day. A few minutes later, the reply came back—short and precise:

"DON'T BE AFRAID OF WHAT WENT WRONG. START BEING POSITVE ABOUT WHAT CAN GO RIGHT."

He and Juliette had a glass of wine and a salad at a quaint little restaurant named 6th & Vine before they went to the movie. Certainly to those sitting at tables near them, they must have seemed to be very mad at each other, or afraid of each other, because they didn't talk. He wanted to speak, but he was incapable. Juliette had questions to ask but seemed unable to.

The longer he looked at her, the more he understood—yet , the more he was perplexed. She would smile and his consciousness would drift into unknown realms. When he gazed into her eyes, her thought processes ceased to work. When it was time to leave for the movie, they both inwardly felt they'd just had the best conversation they'd ever had in their lives. And yet, not a word was uttered.

The movie, "Run For Your Life," was not foreign, but it was forgettable. As they walked outside the theater, he suddenly spoke, saying, "I live nearby. Would you like to sit by the fireplace and talk?" In all her life, Juliette had never been asked to sit by a fireplace and talk. So they did. He asked her about her hopes and dreams. She told him everything. They talked of life, of dance, of happiness and of sadness. They discussed their goals and disappointments. They talked about ideas and events…but they never talked about people.

They stared at the flames in the fireplace, which was a dual fireplace in that it could be used inside and outside on the balcony. They sat outside and listened to the quietness. They listened to the crickets and the owls. They listened to their own heartbeats. They each had never found a companion that was as companionable as the solitude they now enjoyed with each other. They held each other's hands, but no more words were spoken, no more words were needed.

Chapter 8

WHEN JULIETTE WAS BACK AT HER SMALL HOME in the cozy little neighborhood of Ardmore, she made a cup of tea and struggled to understand what had happened. She'd never spent an evening where thoughts and ideas and dreams were discussed, and everything between them was clearly understood. She had no explanation. The usual guys she dated wanted to impress her with how athletic they were, or how intelligent they were, or how funny they were. However, the harder they tried, the less impressed she became. She'd only had one relationship of any substance, which she wished she could forget, but like a nightmare, it kept returning and wouldn't go away.

 Her life as a dancer required almost total commitment of her time and energy. There was very little opportunity for relationships outside the studio. This is the main reason she became involved with Ian, a fellow dancer with the N.C. Dance Theater. She didn't particularly think he was that handsome. He certainly wasn't the smartest guy in the troupe and like a lot of performers, he exhibited a strong tendency towards selfishness and narcissism. However, since the nice looking guys were either gay or dating someone else, Juliette ended up with Ian through a process of elimination. Which was a very sad way to acquire a boyfriend.

When she first went out with Ian, she assumed they were, more or less, just friends spending some time together. However, Ian had other ideas. After all, it wasn't often someone could date a girl as beautiful as Juliette. And in Ian's case—never! He became obsessed with her and very possessive. Unbeknownst to Juliette, he began telling everyone in the dance company that he and Juliette were a couple and deeply in love. For her, Ian was simply someone to talk with and share a cup of coffee with between rehearsals. She really didn't even like him that much. He was a bully. He was loud and obnoxious and treated the janitorial staff like slaves.

The last December that Juliette danced, the whole dance troupe had a big party after the opening night performance of "The Nutcracker" at the Steven's Center. Drinks were flowing. Everyone was happy and joyous and Ian was up to no good. He had been trying for months to have an intimate physical relationship with Juliette. She was not interested in that—not with Ian. In fact, she was on the verge of ending their so-called friendship altogether—his boorish behavior was wearing on her entirely too much.

Ian had acquired, from the friend-of-a-friend-of-a-friend, some sort of drug that when mixed with alcohol, would make the person taking it very groggy and incoherent. At the party, he insisted on bringing Juliette a glass of wine (with the drug he'd added). She had decided to tell Ian that she no longer wanted to see him socially and thought the wine might help her with her courage. It helped alright. It helped her into a semi-state of consciousness, which Ian led everyone to believe was Juliette just being tipsy from the alcohol.

He led her out to his car, drove her to his apartment and carried her to his bedroom. She was unaware of everything. Ian started undressing her and himself, while fondling her in ways he had always dreamed of. Juliette was dimly aware of something happening, but she was still very much in a fog. Then, it seemed to her as though she was alone and very cold. Slowly, her senses started awakening and she felt someone lay down on top of her. She moved her arms and felt bare skin. She felt someone touching her, in places where no one should be touching. This startled her and she opened her eyes and saw Ian's face, and the rest of his naked body—then realized she too was naked.

Juliette screamed. Ian tried to calm her, but she continued to scream until they both heard knocking at Ian's front door. Ian jumped up, grabbed a bath robe and went to the door. Juliette took this moment to grab her dress and the mace from her pocketbook. Somehow, Ian had convinced his neighbor that everything was okay and was walking back into the bedroom when Juliette sprayed him directly in the eyes and face with the mace.

Ian fell to the floor screaming and cursing. Juliette stuffed her bra and underwear into her purse, threw her dress on, grabbed her coat and ran out the door. Fortunately she was able to get away from this monster before anything terrible had happened. Or, so she thought.

What Juliette did not know was that Ian had set up a video recorder in his bedroom and had taped the entire encounter that night. Starting with him undressing her, followed by scenes of him fondling her and posing her as provocatively as he could pose a semi-conscious body. He had intentions of taping the actual sexual encounter as well. Fortunately, before this happened, Juliette woke up enough to realize the circumstances and started screaming. She never saw the recorder when she ran from the bedroom. She thought the nightmare was over. She was wrong.

Chapter 9

AFTER HIS DATE WITH JULIETTE, Abbey was thrown off balance. He was bewildered, dazed, perplexed and discombobulated. He wanted to email his grandfather, but he had no idea how to tell him what he felt or how to ask him what he wanted to know. He only knew that he wanted to hear from him, just to know he was there. If nothing more than to comfort him, to ground him, to get him back into reality. So, he asked his grandfather about life. What had surprised him most about living—now that he's had time to reflect on it for all these years?

He had to wait. 10 minutes. 20 minutes. 30 minutes. This was unusual. His grandfather would normally respond quickly. Finally, after 37 minutes the message came through. Unusual certainly, but upon greater inspection and reflection—quite revealing.

"I THOUGHT GROWING OLD WOULD TAKE LONGER."

Abbey loved his parents, but they were his parents—not his grandfather. They insisted on trying to tell him what to do, where to live, who to see and more importantly, who they thought he should date. His parents came to the United States from India as teenagers to attend school and then college. They came as a single man and woman, even though their marriage had already been arranged and set. As soon as they graduated from college, they would be married and produce offspring—it was the Indian way. Their parents had arranged everything, money had been exchanged, promises were given and it was accepted totally by all involved.

It was not known if his parents attended graduate school after college, and then more post graduate school to earn their doctorate degrees, because they loved education so much, or because they were attempting to put off marriage as long as possible. In any event, they both earned their PhD's and are currently teaching at Appalachian State University in Boone, NC. His father teaches Economics and Applied Statistics and his mother teaches Biology. He is their only child and they constantly worry about him.

From an early age Abhinandan became Americanized, much to his parent's chagrin. He refused to dress in traditional Indian clothes. He did not accept their religious beliefs and social customs and most importantly, he chose who he would date— and it was never a girl of Indian ancestry. This caused his parents many sleepless nights. From his days in high school and into college, it was apparent Abbey possessed a quality that young ladies found appealing. Not only in his good looks, but in his demeanor as well. He was always collected, smooth, confident and intelligent. He never had to look for a girlfriend—he only had to choose which one he wanted.

46

His parents would arrange parties and social events and they always invited several young ladies from inside their Indian social network. He knew what they were trying to do and he was never disrespectful to his parents, but he would not be pushed into any relationships either. He knew what he wanted and who he wanted. All he could do was act naturally.

This was one of the reasons he found comfort and solace in his grandfather. He never tried to push him or persuade him to do anything. He only offered advice and Abbey respected him for that. He would always love his parents and respect them, but he depended on his grandfather for words of wisdom and guidance. His grandfather set an example that he had always admired—he married for love. He ignored the socially acceptable norms of his days when he met and fell in love with Abbey's grandmother, who was from a lower caste than his grandfather. That simply wasn't done in those days. Both were ostracized, both were shunned, both were shamed, but both were extremely happy. Love won.

When he was older, he talked often to his grandfather about what he had given up in order to marry the woman he loved. He knew the caste system in India was rigid and very strict. His grandfather was never sorry about who he married, or what it cost him. He often told Abbey,

"IT'S NOT WHAT WE HAVE IN LIFE, BUT WHO WE HAVE IN OUR LIFE THAT MATTERS."

It was another lesson he never forgot.

He couldn't quit thinking about Juliette. Usually, when he thought about women, he was thinking about "another" woman; not the one he was just with. He didn't understand these feelings. He was more comfortable with things he could visualize, like images on a computer screen. Or, the late afternoon sun reflecting off a smooth, calm lake. The sight of a hawk soaring and circling above. A gentle breeze rustling the leaves on a fall afternoon, or the way a girl flicks the hair off her face. Simple things, tangible things, things he could understand. Not this.

He decided to go to Finnegan's Wake for dinner. He really liked the Blarney Burger and he wanted to see how his friend Opie was doing since the price changes with the beer distributor. The atmosphere at Finnegan's is unlike other bars he's been in—it seems free and easy here—comfortable. Unlike the sour gloom of most bars where nervous men in tight collars are eying querulous women in short dresses. While they each brood over their drinks, watching an English league soccer match on TV. Yet constantly checking their cell phones for emails and texts from someone (anyone) having a better time than they are.

As he sat down and waited for his drink to come, he noticed Opie walking out the front door carrying two Pabst Blue Ribbons. This was curious. Then, two older black men came around the corner carrying brooms. Opie handed each of them a beer, talked a bit, laughed at something and came back inside. He saw Abbey sitting by himself and came up to say hello. He first joked and told him the food here tasted better when sitting beside a beautiful girl. Abbey told him he was indeed working on that situation and hoped to introduce him to a young lady soon.

This caught Opie's attention and he kept bugging him about who this young lady might be. Abbey said, "She's just someone I met from an art gallery downtown." Opie asked, "Juliette?"

Abbey was shocked, "How did you know that? How could you possibly know who she is?"

Opie said, "I've seen the way you look at the blonde Wake Forest girls who come in here. There aren't that many art galleries downtown that have single, attractive blondes —so, it was easy. It had to be Juliette. I've met her before at arts events and merchants associations. She's gorgeous!"

"Yes, she is beautiful. Do you know anything else about her?"

Opie said, "No, I don't know much at all. To be honest, she's too good looking to mess around with any guys I know."

"Maybe that'll change." Abbey said (and hoped). "Opie, can I ask you a personal question?"

"No, I haven't dated Juliette and I don't know if she's good in bed or not."

"Well, that's not exactly what I was going to ask—but, it's good to know." Abbey said, "What I want to ask is why you took beers out to those two old guys sweeping the sidewalk?"

"Oh…those guys live down at the Mission. They're both veterans and as harmless as they can be. I think they collect some sort of pension. I'm not sure, but I am sure they don't have much. It's a little game I play with them. They pretend to sweep the sidewalk in front of the pub and I give them each a beer once a day. It makes them feel good someone cares. It makes me feel even better."

Chapter 10

SUNDAY MORNING, AFTER HE WOKE, Abbey took his laptop and went across the street to Camino's Bakery, the place Juliette had mentioned. He ordered a coffee and cinnamon-raisin bagel, which he took outside to sit at a small table and watch people pass by. Most of the other tables were taken by young professionals or college students who were drawn to the downtown area. He liked people watching, but today he was pre-occupied with Juliette. He checked the website for her gallery, but it didn't include an email address—only information about the exhibits.

He googled her name, but all he found was information on her when she danced—nothing else. He had long before figured out how to access AOL, G-mail, or any other websites people used for email . It was simple enough to enter a name and be directed to the email for that person. He typed in Juliette's name—nothing in any of the servers. Apparently, Juliette was the only person in America without an email address. She had an AOL account, but had closed it several months earlier. He wondered why. He emailed several old friends from Blacksburg, and he answered some emails from work, but he simply couldn't get Juliette off his mind.

As he sat sipping his coffee the laptop dinged with an incoming email from his grandfather. He opened it and it read,

51

"ARE YOU IN CHURCH THIS MORNING?"

He answered, "No Grandfather, I'm still getting settled and haven't looked into my options yet." (This was as unassuming an answer as he could think of at the moment). The reply came back instantly,

"DON'T WAIT TOO LONG."

Abbey wrote back, "I won't. I'm trying to keep an open mind on the entire religion issue." He knew this would elicit a prompt response—and it did,

"THERE IS A DISTINCT DIFFERENCE BETWEEN HAVING AN OPEN MIND AND HAVING A HOLE IN YOUR HEAD FROM WHICH YOUR BRAIN LEAKS OUT."

Now, he had several things to think about. He needed to be alone and contemplate life, religion and the most alluring smile he'd ever imagined. He had seen a brochure around town about a place called "Stone Mountain" near Winston-Salem. He googled it and found that he could drive there in a little over an hour—so he did. After a couple of turns he was on Reynolda Road (named after the tobacco magnet, RJ Reynolds), driving past the opulent Reynolda House and Gardens. Passing by the tree lined entrance to Wake Forest and out of the city he went. Over the Yadkin River and through the small towns of East Bend and Elkin he drove, until he saw the signs for "Stone Mountain State Park."

He parked in the lower lot, gathered his small pack with a water bottle, some raisins, nuts and cheese and started off up the trail. After an hour of climbing, he was at the top of the small mountain. It had a grand view of the surrounding foothills and Blue Ridge Mountains in the distance. It was named "Stone Mountain" because it was just that—all stone on top and down the side. There was very little vegetation where he ended up, just a few little things growing between cracks in the rocks. There were some pine trees on the other side of the mountain. He remembered kicking some pine cones on the way up the trail. He sat next to a boulder and leaned back to enjoy the view—25 miles? 50 miles? 75 miles? He had no idea, but it was nice.

He sat there and thought of everything important. He contemplated the unknown yellow flowers growing in the shade of the boulder. He watched the buzzards soaring above him and below him, riding the thermals off the face of the mountain. He tried to out- stare a blackbird perched on a boulder several yards away. He lost. The silence on top of the mountain was engulfing—nearly deafening. He opened his water bottle and unwrapped some raisins, but the sound it made seemed almost sacrilegious. He dozed off but was awakened by the screeching of a hawk? An owl? Something that had just caught lunch—or just missed catching lunch.

As hard as he tried to think of all things universal, his thoughts keep returning to her smile. Her laugh. Her voice. Her beauty, which was not made of shapes and forms, but shined from within, like a star. All this was enough to make him melt into the bare rock surface of the mountain. He finally rose, trying to shake himself back to inevitability. He took a different route back down the mountain. He heard the tinkling of moving water somewhere in the distance and followed the sound. He passed into a pine forest and saw a doe in the distance with two fawns. He stopped to admire them, they instinctively knew he meant no harm and continued their grazing.

After a few minutes he came upon a large waterfall. He was at the top of the falls and the trail wound itself down to the bottom where it ended in a small pool of water. He took his hiking boots off and dangled his feet in the cool water. He was alone there. He wondered why others weren't there. He wondered about a lot of things—a lot of blonde things in particular.

Abbey had a meeting at the hospital Monday morning with some doctors that had requested a special program be set up for tracking the effects and results of some experimental drugs. Arriving for the meeting, he found the entrance to the hospital blocked by a protest group. Most of the signs they were carrying didn't make sense to him, but one did. It had the name of the experimental drug the doctors were studying written on it. Misspelled—but it was the drug in question. The protesters weren't mad because the drug didn't work, or had bad side effects. They were protesting because the cost of the drug was being increased from $119 per dose, to $750 per dose!

He never got involved in any of the medical issues. His job was to create programs that could track results, predict results and even help doctors to "think" which directions and actions to take. When he finally made it inside to the meeting, the protest outside was the main topic of conversation. Apparently, the drug in question, Quenvestinol, proved to be a major success. Even surpassing what the doctors and inventors of the drug had hoped for. The protesters outside the hospital were the experimental focus group that had been using the drug on their kids. This group of one hundred children had a rare form of cancer and their families had volunteered to be a part of the study to test Quenvestinol .

Other drugs had all proven futile, Quenvestinol had been a miracle drug. Even though the families in the study were given the drug without charge, they knew when the study ended they would then have to buy the drugs, as they would any other drug. They were led to believe the cost of the drug would be $119 per dose—certainly expensive, but one they could somehow manage—if it would save the lives of their children. When the inventor of the drug discovered the overwhelming success of Quenvestinol, they changed the price to $750 per dose, citing cost overruns, production expenses and other medical mishmash.

Hiking the price of drugs, especially new and successful drugs had long been the practice in the medical industry. These manufacturers spent a lot of money in developing new medicines, when they had one that was successful, they needed to cash in on it. The makers of Quenvestinol were ready to cash in. It was a German company, Siegenthorpe, which had worldwide sales in the billions of dollars. They were familiar with protesters. They weren't concerned with protesters—they were concerned about the bottom line.

After the meeting, Abbey had to walk near the protest group to enter the parking garage. As he did a young woman came running up to him pleading for him to stop. He really had no choice but to hear what she had to say. She cried, "Doctor, you've got to help me." Abbey, being dressed better than any doctor would think about dressing, said, "I'm sorry, but I'm not a doctor. Is something wrong? Should I call someone for you?" She replied, "I just thought you were one of the doctors. I need to speak to someone. My son is sick and taking this drug and now they're going to hike up the price and I can't afford it. What am I supposed to do? Just let him die?"

The more he tried to tell her he wasn't a doctor, she more she pleaded with him to help her and her son. He tried to walk away. She kept following him, crying and pleading. As he was about to enter the parking garage, she suddenly grabbed his arm and collapsed. Frantically, he started screaming for help. He was so close to the hospital, yet no one to help. Finally, a security guard heard him and found an EMS vehicle that was leaving the hospital. They rushed over. Apparently, the woman was just overcome with emotion and had fainted. It scared him…it scared him good.

Chapter 11

AFTER WORK THAT NIGHT, he investigated Siegenthorpe's website, which made them seem like Mother Theresa, Gandhi, Martin Luther King and Nelson Mandela all rolled up into one nice, corporate package. Their website extolled the virtues of Siegenthorpe's vast array of networks and humanitarian goals. They were indeed worldwide, covering all six continents. Trying to follow the revenues of such a vast corporation was nearly impossible—they were just too big. He had to think about this awhile.

He changed clothes and was hanging up his suit coat, when he felt something in the pocket. Inside, he found a card the young woman had slipped in his pocket when she grabbed his arm at the hospital. It was a note that simply said,

"Please help me. My son will die without help. Please!

Annie Norwood"

He didn't know what to do. He didn't know what he could do. But he wanted to do something—anything. When he was perplexed, like now, it always made him feel better to write to his grandfather for advice—so he did.

In the morning, he eagerly opened his email to find this message,

"DO SOMETHING TODAY THAT YOUR FUTURE SELF
WILL THANK YOU FOR."

The message simply reinforced what he already knew. He had
to do something—but what?

First, he'd try to find out as much as possible about Annie
Norwood. He checked into the Forsyth County tax records and
found no house or land listed in her name. But she did have a
car listed, a 2005 Jeep—nothing else. He then hacked back into
the IRS (which was entirely too easy) and found her tax listings
for last year. Annie had worked two jobs, one at The District, a
local restaurant that had recently closed. And another job at a
local rest home in King, NC. She made $12,475 as a waitress
and $10,120 as a nurse's helper at the rest home.

Her address was at a low-income apartment complex in the
city's south side. After taxes, he was pretty certain that she
could barely make rent payments, buy food and life's essentials
for herself and her child. A 400-500% raise in the cost of
medicines for her son simply was not possible for her. All day
Sunday he thought. Siegenthorpe seemed too good to be true.
He checked all their links, all their subsidiaries and the top
officers of the corporation. He couldn't find anything.

This was discouraging. He didn't know where to turn. The
company made great products, was a model corporate citizen,
donated to all sorts of charities and organizations. Wait a
minute! He recognized about 75% of these donations, but just
who was receiving the rest of the money? There were fourteen
listings for charitable donations which he didn't recognize. The
odd thing about these was that thirteen of the fourteen received
about the same amount from Seigenthorpe. But the fourteenth
received more than eight times the amount the others did.
Why? There had to be a reason. He had to find out. Quickly.

It was very frustrating for him. The donation listing for "The White Dove Foundation" described it as a charitable organization whose sole purpose was to help those displaced by famine or war in the Middle East. Their website listed a President and Board of Directors and not much else. Their address was in Zurich, Switzerland. The Swiss, who valued their privacy above all else, had one of the safest and most secure systems in the world. But Abbey had one of the brightest and most intelligent minds in the world. It took him a few hours, but he got in—totally unnoticed by their firewalls and security systems.

He looked at the corporate account of "The White Dove Foundation" and indeed found where Seigenthorpe had deposited money into their account. What was odd was that in every single instance where money had been deposited, within an hour, the same amount of money had been transferred out of that account into the personal account of the President of "The White Dove Foundation." His name was Amir al-Thani, who listed his nationality as Swiss.

He was indeed a Swiss citizen, Abbey found, for all of four years. Before that, he had addresses in Libya, Syria and Iran. He was educated at the London School of Economics and at Oxford and had held a variety of jobs in the governments of several Arab countries. How he became President of "The White Dove Foundation" was unclear. What was clear was that in the last four years, Seigenthorpe had deposited over $37 million dollars into "The White Dove Foundation." And every cent of that money was then transferred into the personal account of Amir al-Thani. One didn't have to possess the intuitive skills of Sherlock Holmes to conclude something was very fishy in these waters.

He tried all night to follow the money from al-Thani but it kept leading to dead ends. Apparently the money just disappeared. It didn't stay in his personal account long. He didn't have any investments out of the ordinary. His apartment in Zurich was modest, he lived an unassuming lifestyle. By all accounts, he was a very ordinary, if not boring, executive. Too boring and too ordinary is what Abbey thought. Someone who had over $37 million dollars would do something with it. They would buy something—do something—anything. But not al-Thani.

He was at a dead end. There was nowhere else to look, nowhere to go. The money came into the accounts of "The White Dove Foundation", transferred to al-Thani and then vanished. Abbey didn't like to lose. He finally went to bed trying to think blonde thoughts, trying to conjure up that alluring smile that had so devastated him. He couldn't. His mind could not cease its thoughts of White Dove, al-Thani and 37 million un-accounted for dollars.

Maybe for the first time in his life, he was distracted at work. He couldn't stop thinking about Seigenthorpe and the $37 million. That money went somewhere—somewhere that Seigenthorpe and al-Thani didn't want known. This, he was certain of.

He went back to Seigenthorpe's website, hacked into the financial side and copied information which meant nothing to him, but he did it to prove to Seigenthorpe that he had been in their system. If he could convince them he knew some of their secrets, maybe he could bluff his way into scaring them that he knew ALL their secrets.

He then gathered private information from the President of Seigenthorpe and several of the Board of Directors as well. Nothing of consequence—they were all too sterile for that. He only gathered information so that they knew he COULD gather information. If he could get this stuff—what else would he be able to see? This was the bluff he wanted to play.

He found the private email address for the President, a man named Conrad Dixon, who lived in Paris. He copied all the financial and personal information he had gathered from Seigenthorpe, Conrad Dixon and several board members and sent it to Mr. Dixon via a secure and totally anonymous email router that made stops in Amsterdam, Reykjavik, Guam and Buenos Aires before it ended at the Paris home of Mr. Dixon.

The email read, "This information is the tip of the iceberg. I know everything about your company and you. However, the only thing I care about is the money al-Thani is dispersing. I only want two things from you: First, al-Thani ceases his private funding. Second, you significantly raised the price of a drug called Quenvestinol in the United States. I want you to stop this price increase and keep the drug at its original price. If both these demands aren't met immediately, I will send the information about your donations to al-Thani and what he is doing with that money to every major newspaper in the world. You have until Friday."

Abbey had no idea what al-Thani did with the $37 million. But, a man with ties to several Arab countries and this money apparently disappearing could lead to some very disturbing scenarios. He was sure Conrad Dixon did not want this information becoming public. This was his bluff. He could only wait now.

Thursday morning, on the second page of the Winston- Salem Journal, there was a short article announcing that the drug maker Seigenthorpe had decided to keep the price of its new drug, Quenvestinol, at its original price, $119, instead of the proposed new cost of $750. New production techniques would enable them to control the costs and keep the drug at its present structure. The company was very happy to be able to do this for its American market.

When he read this, he then googled "The White Dove Foundation" and found a small article in the Zurich papers announcing that "The White Dove Foundation" had ceased operations and had closed its offices. No explanations. He leaned back in his chair and thought, "Sometimes, it's fun being me."

Chapter 12

IT HAD BEEN A FEW DAYS since he emailed his grandfather. He'd been consumed with Seigenthorpe. But his grandfather hadn't forgotten him. This message was waiting for him in the morning,

"SEEK OPPORTUNITIES TO SHOW YOU CARE. THE SMALLEST GESTURES OFTEN MAKE THE BIGGEST DIFFERENCE."

He had forgotten to ask Juliette for her home phone number. He was so used to emailing everyone that phoning was nearly foreign to him. He tried calling the gallery a couple of times, but she was never in. He couldn't understand why she didn't have email or even a cell phone. Apparently everyone else in the world had a cell phone—except Juliette. Very strange.

The reason Juliette gave up her email account and her cell phone was very simple—Ian. Juliette had not spoken to Ian after that dreadful night where he tried to dope her, rape her and tape the entire incident. But he had harassed her with phone calls, emails and texts. This is the reason she discontinued all those services. She finally had to get a restraining order from the police to keep him from coming around the gallery and stalking her.

He had left threatening, anonymous notes telling her that she should never see anyone else. That they were made for each other and would one day be together. He was truly delusional... and scary. She found a dead cat once on her doorstep. She couldn't prove it was Ian's work. But she knew it was him. The tires on her car were slashed another time. The front of the gallery had been spray painted once with the word "Slut" in bright red letters.

She answered the phone in the gallery one day to hear Ian's voice. He told her if she EVER dated anyone else but him, they would both be sorry. She quickly hung up and would not answer the phone any longer. This is why Abbey couldn't reach her.

He left work a couple of hours early Friday with the intention of getting to the gallery before it closed. Usually, in his life, it was the woman chasing him. This was very unusual, him doing the pursuing. But he couldn't help it. He'd go anywhere, do anything to see that smile again. He drove down 4th Street and found a parking space between Foothill's Brewery and the gallery. He pulled in the space, turned the car off, got out and realized he didn't have any quarters for the parking meter.

He saw two men walking down the street carrying back packs. He thought they might be homeless, so he stopped them and offered them $5.00 if they would give him a couple of quarters. They weren't homeless. They were just a couple of guys going down to Gold's Gym on the corner. They didn't have any quarters. He ran across the street to the Chamber of Commerce building , but the receptionist seemed more scared than helpful. It wasn't often a well dressed, handsome Indian man barged in the office requesting two quarters. She didn't have any. She offered him a dollar bill.

He'd heard that if you didn't pay the parking meter, the city would tow your car away. He didn't know if this was true or not. Maybe it was just another urban tale, like the one of Batman being seen on the tops of several buildings downtown. Not the cartoon character, but a real person, dressed like Batman, standing on the edges of several rooftops in the downtown area. At any rate, he didn't want his car towed away, so he headed back up the street towards his vehicle to move it.

As he walked up to his car, he saw an older, gray-headed man, sort of tall and thin, putting quarters in his meter for him. He walked up to him and the man turned and said, "Don't worry about it son, I got this one." Except for "Thank you," Abbey didn't know what to say. He just smiled and walked toward the gallery, feeling good about himself, Winston-Salem and mankind.

He walked up to the gallery window and looked in. Juliette was on a stool, trying to hang a metal sculpture from the wall. She had on a flowery dress and every time she reached up, the dress would rise a few inches up her legs. She'd reach up to hammer and the dress would rise. She'd reach up to measure and the dress would rise. By the time she reached up to actually hang the sculpture, Abbey had nearly fainted. He hadn't realized just how beautiful she was, nor had he realized how magnificent her legs were. Years of dancing had obviously firmed and shaped her body into incredible dimensions.

He had to back down the street and compose himself. He found a chair and a small table and sat down, thinking about the vision he'd just seen. He was completely lost in his thoughts of long and shapely legs when someone tapped him on the shoulder. "Can I take your order?" He looked up, then he looked at the sign for Skippy's Hot Dogs. "Oh no," he said, "I'm sorry. I was just resting, I'll be leaving now." The young waitress smiled and said, "That's okay, stay as long as you like. Let me know if you need anything."

He thought, "What kind of spell does this woman have on me? I can't think or talk and now I can't even stand up!"

He decided to sit there at Skippy's and wait for Juliette to leave the gallery at closing time. The young waitress came around again and he smiled at her and asked what her name was. She blushed and said her name was Anna. When she composed herself she asked what his name was and if he wanted to order anything. He ordered a Diet Coke. She wrote it down, then looked at him again and asked the same three questions he was asked a hundred times a day: "Where are you from? Are you American?" And, "How do you spell your name?" He answered all three as politely as he could—it wasn't easy.

He sat there watching the traffic and the people go by, waiting for Juliette to close her shop and walk out the door. He was good at waiting—it gave his mind time to wander. He thought of tangible things. Things he could touch and feel: the course texture of the bare rock on Stone Mountain, the incredible smoothness on the inside of a woman's thigh, the bark of an old oak tree, the calloused hands of his grandfather, or the smooth skin of a grape just plucked from the vine. The alluring smile of Juliette distracted him and bewildered him. He wondered how something he couldn't feel or touch could affect him so. He had no answer. No computer program would ever be able to solve this for him.

Chapter 13

HE WAS DEEP IN HIS THOUGHTS when Juliette came out of the gallery and locked the doors. She saw him sitting at the table in front of Skippy's and walked up to him, tapped him on the shoulder and said, "Are you hungry?" "Um, no. I was just....um, I was going to...I was just having a drink." Stammering like a fool was not in his DNA. The physical sight of her turned him into a blabbering idiot. She said, "I was hoping you were hungry so we could go to dinner together, but, if you're not hungry, then...."

"Oh no, I am hungry. I mean I wasn't hungry then, but I will be." At least that didn't sound too absurd. They started walking down the street, casually glancing at each other, while not knowing exactly what to say. Finally, he said, "It's been a beautiful day." Juliette stopped , turned to face him, leaned up and kissed him on the cheek, then continued walking as she said, "Yes, it has been Abhinandan." With that kiss, he couldn't feel his feet touching the sidewalk any longer. All he could think was somehow, "I've got to get you into my life."

They walked a couple of blocks to Mozelle's, which specializes in Southern cuisine. He ordered the Southern spring rolls, pulled pork, napa cabbage, collards with sesame ginger. Juliette ordered the tomato bisque soup, with a fried goat cheese salad. They ordered a bottle of Shelton's Riesling to go with dinner. The wine put him at ease (a little). They talked of nothing—and of everything. He would've been content to simply look into her eyes and melt every time she smiled at him. Abbey knew from experience that every woman is a mystery to be solved. Only now, the mystery seemed to elude him.

They shared a slice of key lime pie and had a cup of coffee before they walked back to her car. As they walked from the restaurant, Abbey thought he could live happily forever, simply lying helplessly in her arms. Juliette took his hand as they walked and dreamed that a single soul born in heaven, could split into twin spirits and shoot like falling stars into earth, where over oceans and continents their magnetic forces would finally unite them back onto one. How else to explain this feeling? How else to explain this love?

As they got close to her car, she suddenly became rigid. He was preparing to ask her to go over to Finnegan's with him for a drink when she said, "Thank you Abhinandan. Dinner was wonderful, I'm so glad you got your appetite back. I hope you'll call me again soon." And without any hesitation, she opened her car door, got in and drove away. He was left standing there wondering what had just happened.

Something had indeed happened. As they were nearly to her car, Juliette saw Ian sitting in a parked car across the street staring at her. Why wouldn't this maniac leave her alone? What was he going to do now? Should she call the police? These, and many other questions, were flooding her mind. Until she pulled in her driveway and got out of her car, she hadn't noticed the small slip of paper underneath the passenger side wiper blade. She knew who put it there. She hated to even touch it. But she did.

It read: "I warned you. Do you want me to hurt him? It's up to you." It was a typed message, unsigned, written by a deranged, warped mind. She ran inside and locked the doors. She was frantic and knew she couldn't keep living like this. Now, she was jeopardizing Abbey, someone who was completely innocent and oblivious to anything going on.

He went back to his condo perplexed, excited, confused, bewildered and uncertain of what had happened this evening. A great dinner, wonderful conversation, that beautiful smile…then, apparently out of nowhere, she changed. He thought, "Did I do something? Did I say something wrong? Am I missing something?" There weren't many things that could confound him. This one was driving him crazy.

He wrote a long, rambling email to his grandfather, not really asking for advice, but detailing his feelings. Venting. Even though it was a work night, the thought of going to bed seemed absurd. He went out to the balcony searching for solace in the sounds of the night. The comforting symphony of crickets , locusts and owls that had always eased his mind in the past, did little for him tonight. If it had been any other woman, he would simply walk away. If it had been any other woman, he wouldn't think twice about it. But it wasn't any other woman. It was her. It was that smile. That voice. Those legs. He was hooked and there was no wriggling off the line now.

After a few uncomfortable hours in bed, he rose, turned on the Keurig and checked his emails. There was only one he wanted to open, it read,

"THERE'S NOTHING SO BAD THAT IT COULDN'T BE WORSE."

Chapter 14

ABBEY HAD TO ATTEND A CEREMONY AT LUNCH being held at Ryan's Steak House by his company. It was to celebrate a new contract they'd just signed with Novant Health to provide technical help and software for all Novant's offices throughout the southeast. What he didn't know was that it also was an opportunity for the President of Lonewolf Enterprises to recognize the work he had done on this project and to present him with a bonus. It was chiefly Abbey's work that had secured the new contract with Novant and the president wanted to publicly recognize him and give him a bonus check for $25,000.

This was a nice surprise, even nicer was when the president told him to take the rest of the week off. Somehow, the president thought all the work Abbey was doing had been taxing on him and he wanted to keep his prize employee fresh and happy. In fact, the new programs he had developed were common sense ideas that should have been done years earlier. He wondered why nobody had come up with this idea sooner. The reason was simple...no one had the mind Abbey had. No one thought like he did.

He needed to get away and think... not about work, about Juliette. When at Virginia Tech he'd seen billboards and advertisements for Harrah's Casino in Cherokee, N.C. He had never been to a casino before, but he liked to play cards. In his mind it was easy for him to calculate odds in card games and play the percentages. In local games amongst his friends he'd always won a few dollars each time they played. He didn't care about the money. He liked the challenge and the inner game of "reading" his opponents.

Now that he had received a bonus, he wanted to try his luck and skill at a casino and see if his card theories and skills worked there, like they did in games with his friends. He made the drive to Cherokee up through the Blue Ridge Mountains, which always seemed to relax him. The vistas and overlooks had a way of uncluttering his mind of nearly everything (except blonde thoughts). He checked in for two nights, ate dinner at the buffet and walked around trying to familiarize himself with the casino and the layout.

He found the card room and was relieved there were several tables devoted solely to his favorite game, No-limit Texas Hold'em. The rules of this game were simple. It took only a few minutes for someone to learn, but a lifetime for anyone to master. He had the foresight and wisdom to know that in Texas Hold'em, you didn't play the cards, you played the players. And nobody read people better than him.

This was a game where each of the players was dealt two cards apiece. Then each person was permitted to either fold their cards, check –and make no bet, or bet on the two cards they had. After this, some people folded, some people checked and maybe one or two would bet that the two cards they held were the best two cards at the table. Then, three community cards would be dealt (the flop) and another round of betting would ensue where people could either "call" that bet, raise the bet, or fold their hand.

After this, a fourth card (the turn) and a fifth card (the river) would be dealt, one at a time, with bets made on each card. Then a final bet would be made and the person who had the best hand would win the pot. Since this game was "no limit", it meant the pots could be as few as $10-$20, or up to several thousand dollars. It was not necessarily a game of having the best hand, or of bluffing that you had the best hand. Most importantly, it was a game of reading your opponents to tell if they were bluffing you. This is where Abbey excelled.

He played very conservatively at first, reading his opponents. Learning small "signs" each of them showed—but didn't know they were showing. One player might unconsciously rub his nose if he had a good hand, another might have a small twitch if he was bluffing. Some others may slightly blush if they had Aces, where someone else's eyes might dilate if they had a strong hand. He saw (and read) all these little nuances of his opponents, which he stored away in his mind to use at the appropriate time.

He stayed away from the big pots until he was sure he had correct "reads" on all the other players. When he was pretty certain about what he was seeing, he joined the big money hands. He soon started winning a lot more than the other players. Some were getting frustrated and some good old boys were a little mad that this "foreigner" was taking their money—at their own game!

After several hours of playing he was up about $3,100 and had decided to call it a night after a couple more hands. There was one middle-aged guy at the table, wearing a big cowboy hat— the kind that had the front brim and back brim bent down significantly. He kept running his mouth all evening, not at Abbey, but to the other players about him. Calling it "beginner's luck," saying to no one in particular that this was an "American game." He would talk loudly to his friends referring to Abbey as a "foreigner" and even once used the term "rag-head." Abbey sat there—taking it all in. Reading all the signs and tells of the other players.

Finally, the good old boy, who went by the name of "Dusty," got a hand and pushed half of his chips in the pot. He said, "Here you go boys. Let's see who's got the balls to hang with me on this hand." Everyone else immediately folded their cards—except Abbey. He never looked at the two cards that had been dealt him. He kept his gaze on Dusty. After about thirty seconds, Abbey said, "I call your bet and double the raise." The other players were stunned. Dusty looked at him and said, "How can you make that kind of raise? You haven't even looked at your cards." Abbey replied, "I don't need to look at my cards, all I need to know is what YOU have. And you don't have squat!"

No one spoke. No one even moved. The dealer finally looked at Dusty and said, "It's your play sir."

Without speaking, Dusty threw his cards towards the dealer, pushed his chair back, got up and walked away without another word, forfeiting the substantial pot to Abbey. No one saw what two cards Dusty held. No one was brave enough to ask Abbey what two cards he held. All they knew was that none of them wanted to play this man for any big money—EVER!

He was too keyed up to sleep. He went to a bar at the casino, ordered an Iron Maiden and sat at a corner table to think and unwind. He wanted to call Juliette—but couldn't (she had no phone). He wanted his mind to stop racing—it wouldn't. He wanted to understand what had changed Juliette so much on their walk to her car a few nights earlier—but he couldn't. He wanted to understand what had changed in him—but was unable.

As he was waiting to pay his bill for the drink, a well dressed Asian man came up to his table and introduced himself as Mr. Wong. He asked if he could join him for a minute or two—he didn't wait for Abbey to answer before he sat down. He said he'd observed his play in the casino and was impressed. He invited him to play at his table in the "high stakes" poker room.

It took Abbey about three seconds to size up Mr. Wong. He was a professional gambler and obviously a high stakes player. He wasn't sure he wanted to get involved with professionals, but he was confident in his abilities and intrigued with Mr. Wong's invitation. He looked at him and said, "I'm not sure a beginner and novice like me is capable of playing in the high stakes room with you sir. I feel like you'd try to take all my money if I went in there. Wouldn't you?"

Wong looked back at him and replied, "I'd certainly try to, but I've watched you play. You're no novice, nor a beginner—you know what you're doing. But I'd still probably take your money."

Sometimes Abbey couldn't help himself. This was one of those times. He stared directly into Wong's eyes and said, "I'm sure you'd try sir, but I doubt very seriously that would happen." As soon as he spoke those words, he wished he'd had them back. Wong hesitated a moment then rose and said, "We shall see about that my friend. We shall see." Wong walked away. Abbey sat there wondering why he couldn't keep his mouth shut.

He went back to his room and opened his laptop. As usual, there was a message from his grandfather. It read,

"THE TWO MOST IMPORTANT DAYS OF YOUR LIFE ARE ONE, WHEN YOU ARE BORN. AND TWO, WHEN YOU FIGURE OUT WHY YOU WERE BORN."

Again, it was a message he didn't quite understand initially. Then, on second thought, it was one that made perfect sense to him. Finally, something that made sense. Maybe he could go to sleep now.

Having won a little over $6,000 at the poker table, he decided that was enough. He cut his stay short in Cherokee and decided to make the drive along the Blue Ridge Parkway over to Grandfather Mountain. He'd been there as a boy and the name of the place was always special to him, "Grandfather." As usual, the drive through the valleys and peaks was spectacular. The winding roads made him concentrate on driving rather than other more alluring thoughts.

He stopped at the mountain, walked across the "mile high swinging bridge" and visited the bear's habitat. (They were sleeping). He then found a bench and sat down to let his mind wander without thinking about driving. He needed time to get his mind off his troubles and think about other things. After a few hours of staring at the peaks and valleys of Appalachia, he started driving again and found a small bed-and-breakfast near Asheville where he spent the night. He woke up early the next morning with the usual email from his grandfather that had him returning to the message in his mind, over and over. It said,

"STRIVE NOT TO BE A SUCCESS, BUT RATHER TO BE OF VALUE."

He was successful at poker last night. Now he wanted that success to be of value. The money was great, but it didn't really mean a lot to him. It was more of a reward for proving to himself he could read people and their intentions. However, the money would be of great value to Annie Norwood, the woman who left the note in his pocket at the picket line that day. He could not forget her pleas for help and the urgency in her voice.

When he got back to Winston-Salem, he went to the bank and got a Cashier's check for $4,432 and made it out to Annie Norwood. He then addressed an envelope to her, put the check in and mailed it—with no return address. Then he went to Lefkowitz Tailor Shop and ordered a custom- made suit of the finest material available. A new suit always soothed his soul. This had been a great day.

Chapter 15

JULIETTE WAS AT HER WIT'S END. She had never met anyone quite like Abbey and she thought about him all day long. She'd never met anyone who just wanted to "be" with her, someone who was thrilled to sit around and talk with her. Someone who was interested in what she thought and in what she said. Someone who's sole purpose was not to "bed" her as fast as possible. In short, she'd never met anyone like Abbey.

Now, she has this maniac Ian threatening not only her, but Abbey as well. Should she go to the police? (She doesn't have any definitive proof to give them.) Any notes she has are typed and are not signed. She calls her mom, and tells about someone stalking her and some of the things this man has done, and is still doing. Of course, her mother is frantic and scared for her daughter. She insists Juliette close the shop and come home to California before something truly tragic happens.

Juliette is torn. Winston-Salem is her home—she loves it there. But living in the same town with Ian might be impossible. And, apparently, she's now dragging Abbey into all her mess. It's almost too much to bear. After thinking about it all, she finally relents and tells her mother she'll come home for a visit—of unknown duration—so she can sort things out. Her mother makes reservations for Juliette to leave that night out of Greensboro, changing planes in Atlanta, then straight through to San Francisco.

Juliette arranged for her assistant to run the gallery in her absence. She didn't tell her, or anyone else, where she was going, only that she'd be away for awhile. She didn't want to take the chance that Ian could find out from anyone where she was. She packed her suitcases, called a taxi and she was gone. She thought about calling Abbey, but since she didn't have a phone, or his number, she didn't. Plus, she thought it would be safer for him not to know. She cried all the way to the airport.

Juliette had never wanted anyone to know who her parents were. Her dad was very well known in California's elite social circles and financial circles. Juliette never wanted her success as a dancer to be because people knew who her father was, so she always used her mother's maiden name as her own last name. Therefore, anyone trying to trace Juliette McGranahan would find no evidence of that name anywhere in the country, except in Winston-Salem. For all intents and purposes, Juliette was now invisible.

Abbey awoke feeling very good about himself and his station in life. He brewed some coffee, fired up his laptop and sat down to review the overnight emails—one in particular, which read,

"IN LIFE, IT'S NOT WHERE YOU GO—IT'S WHO GOES WITH YOU."

He knew exactly who he wanted to go with him right now....Juliette. He had never been in love before, but he thought he might be headed down that road right now. Since he was on his last day off from work, he thought he'd go down to Camino's Bakery and get a couple of pastries and some coffee and surprise Juliette at her gallery. He really liked the sweet rolls, but he noticed Juliette had plain bagels with him before, so he compromised and ordered two blueberry scones.

He walked in the front and saw Juliette's assistant, Martha, dusting some paintings on the wall. She was always doing something like that whenever he was around—like she couldn't sit still. She looked at him and said hello and he said, "Is Juliette in the back?" Martha said, "No, I'm afraid she's not here right now." "When do you think she'll be back Martha?" Martha looked at him, then looked at the floor, then fidgeted and finally said, "I'm not sure. It might be awhile."

"What do you mean, it might be awhile?" Again, Martha seemed bothered and unsure what to say. Abbey said, "Martha, if there's something you need to tell me, just go ahead. Is Juliette sick or something?" As Martha looked at him, tears swelled in her eyes and she said, "She's gone! She left with no explanation. She didn't tell me where she was going or how long she'd be away."

It took him a few moments for this information to register. He said, "Did she leave a number or any contact information?" "No." He asked, "Do you know why she left so suddenly? " Again, Martha said, "No." "What else can you tell me Martha?" "I'm sorry, I wish I knew something else. It's totally unlike her to just leave like this." He could tell Martha was on the verge of tears and didn't know anything else about what happened. He wrote his phone number on a card and asked Martha to call him if she heard anything. He didn't know if she would call or not, but he couldn't think of anything else. He left the scones and the coffee on the counter and walked outside, not knowing which way to go, or what to do.

The only thing he could think of was to go back to his condo and start a complete on-line search for Juliette. All he could find was information from Winston-Salem. Her lease on the store, her home, things of that nature. He couldn't find anything substantial—and he tried. He remembered she told him she was originally from California, but he could not find any history of her through tax records, the DMV or any medical information. It was as though Juliette McGranahan had simply materialized in Winston-Salem....and had now vanished.

Chapter 16

HE DIDN'T KNOW WHAT TO THINK. Should he be worried? Was she only visiting a friend? Had he said something or done something? He had no idea. Since he could find no trace of Juliette on-line, he was at a dead end. He decided to simply wait and see what happened. Maybe this was nothing more than a young lady needing to get away for a few days.

He changed his clothes, put on his finest tennis attire and went to Hanes Park to hit some tennis balls. He enjoyed the consistency of the ball machine. He had beautiful strokes and caught the attention of several on-lookers, as well as the pro in the tennis shop. Hitting balls came rather naturally to him and before he realized what had happened, he noticed he was sweating. This was unacceptable. Thoughts of Juliette had entirely pre-occupied his mind, and the rhythm of the ball machine had nearly mesmerized him.

He had stopped to gather his thoughts (and to stop this ridiculous perspiration) when the tennis pro came up to the fence and introduced himself. "You have some very nice strokes. I can tell you've played a lot." "No. Actually I never play," Abbey said, "I'm just here for some exercise." The pro said, "Well, you must've played sometime. You're too good."

He was in no mood for this chitchat or meaningless conversation, so he looked at him and replied, "I didn't say I

COULDN'T play; I said I DON'T play." And with that, he turned and walked away, leaving the pro to contemplate this strange turn of events. The young pro decided he'd be better off going back into the pro shop and stringing some rackets. He'd also learned a valuable lesson years ago from his grandfather, "Being kind is more important than being right."

As he was walking back to his car, Abbey felt badly for being curt and short with the young tennis pro. This wasn't him. Juliette had him all flustered and askew. He went back to his condo, opened a bottle of Placid Peach, from Weathervane Winery, and sat on his balcony contemplating the view and the mystery of Pilot Mountain.

He stayed in his funk for nearly three weeks. No word came from Juliette. It was as if she were an apparition that he'd imagined, then suddenly awoke and she was gone. But, he knew she was real. He knew that smile would forever break his heart and melt his soul. He was lost and didn't know where to turn for help. Finally, he outlined his feelings and circumstances in a long email to his grandfather. He had no idea what type of response he would receive. He'd never really discussed affairs of the heart with him before. It took longer than usual for the reply to come back from India. Abbey was hesitant to open it, afraid of what it might say. But he did—this is what his grandfather told him:

"MY SON, YOU WILL MEET MANY WOMEN IN YOUR LIFE AND YOU WILL FORGET ALMOST EVERYTHING

THEY SAY. AND, YOU'LL ALSO FORGET EVERYTHING THEY DO. BUT, IF YOU'RE LUCKY, YOU MAY MEET ONE WOMAN WHO YOU'LL NEVER FORGET HOW SHE MADE YOU FEEL. CHASE HER TO THE END OF THE EARTH.

LOOK TO WHERE LOVE IS GOING TO BE, NOT WHERE IT USED TO BE. IF YOU NEED ME, CALL ME. I DON'T CARE IF I'M SLEEPING, IF I'M HAVING MY OWN PROBLEMS OR IF I'VE BEEN ANGRY AT YOU. IF YOU NEED ME AND IF YOU NEED TO TALK, I'LL ALWAYS BE THERE FOR YOU. NO MATTER HOW BIG OR SMALL YOUR PROBLEM IS…I'LL BE THERE."

He decided to go to church on Sunday to honor his grandfather's wishes. There was a small Moravian church near Old Salem and this is where he went. He truly had no clue what Moravians were or what they believed. But he went. He was met at the door by some very friendly people and led down a few pews and seated next to a woman who looked to be at least 90 years old—except that she had red hair. Very red hair.

She looked at this handsome foreigner seated next to her, cocked her head slightly and said, "I don't think you're from around here are you?" He playfully replied, "No ma'am, I'm not….I live downtown." She smiled a little crooked smile and said, "I thought so—slide over a little closer to me."

She said, "I'm glad you're here with us today. Do you think you'll be joining our church?" Abbey replied, "Well, I'm not sure. To be quite honest, I don't really know what Moravians believe in." She looked back at him and said, "It's really quite simple…preach the Gospel at all times; use words if necessary."

"I'm Mrs. Carter." She said. He smiled at her and replied, "My name is Abhinandan." But before he could spell it for her, she cocked her head again and asked, "Is that spelled A b h I n a n d a n?" Totally surprised, he answered, "Yes, indeed it is." "I thought so." She said. And the choir started singing, "Lord, I'm Coming Home."

After the hymns were sung and the offering collected, Mrs. Carter fell fast asleep during the sermon. She awoke, as if on cue, in time for the invitation and closing hymn. As they got up to leave the service, he asked her if she needed any help. She looked up at him and said, "Well, you could smile at me again." Ninety years old, yet she was not immune. He smiled and promised he'd be back to see her.

He went back to his condo and typed a message to his grandfather telling him he'd been to church. He first told him how work was progressing and what he was working on. He caught him up on his parents and his personal life, then he ended his message, "I attended church today, hoping to be more like you."

He knew this last missive would elicit a prompt response. It did,

"NOBODY CAN BE EXACTLY LIKE ME. SOMETIMES EVEN I HAVE TROUBLE DOING IT."

Chapter 17

JULIETTE WAS MET AT SAN FRANCISCO'S AIRPORT by her mom and they drove back to their house in Tiburon. On the drive, Juliette tried to explain what was happening with Ian as best as she could, but decided to leave out the part about the drugging and attempted rape. She just told her mom she felt as though she was being stalked and felt uncomfortable.

Her mom and dad lived in a gated community and it was evident her parents had done well financially through earnings and investing. They gave Juliette the entire upstairs, which included three bedrooms, two full baths, a living area and a small in-house gym. Her parent's bedroom was downstairs as was her younger brother's bedroom, which was vacant now since he was away at Stanford. But still, Juliette noticed the maid making up the bed and dusting in the bedroom occasionally.

Juliette didn't know what to do with her time. She was used to being busy with the gallery and with social functions with the School of the Arts and the Dance Theatre. She had no plans, other than to escape from Ian and his craziness. She wrote a letter to Abbey every day. And every day, she tore it up. Certainly, he didn't feel about her the way she felt about him.

She called Martha to check on the gallery and answered work related questions. She would not and did not answer any of the questions Martha asked about where she was and how long she'd be gone. She wasn't sure if Martha was genuinely concerned, or was scared of being on her own. Martha wasn't the most confident and stable employee Juliette could have hired, but she liked her.

Almost from the outset, her parents started arranging parties and dances and lunches and social gatherings trying to ease Juliette into their social circles and introducing her to the most eligible bachelors of Marin County. All the men were nice. All the men were rich. All the men were talented and confident and successful. But none of the men were Abbey.

None of the men had ever asked her if she wanted to sit by a fire and talk. None of them had that quality, had that essence, that substance, core and embodiment he possessed. That unknown attribute that couldn't be described or ever be matched.

She dutifully went to dinners, danced with everyone at the parties, laughed at all the stories and cried herself to sleep every night. She was beginning to think Abbey may have been her one and only chance at happiness and love. Now, he was three thousand miles away in distance and a million miles away in reality. So, she cried.

He checked with Martha at the gallery every few days. Martha always told him she hadn't heard anything from Juliette. He knew she was lying. She knew that he knew she was lying. But neither of them could do anything but continue this little game they were playing. Abbey, because he simply couldn't stop—or give up. Martha, because she valued her job and friendship with Juliette.

Abbey continued amazing Lonewolf Enterprises with his innovations. Novant Health was eagerly waiting on every new program and concept he came up with. The President of Lonewolf was concerned that either Novant or one of the big hospitals would try to lure him away. His main concern was to keep Abbey happy, challenged and on his payroll.

He was told to "Work on whatever pleases you, whatever your mind thinks of, whatever challenges you." He had an office, but most days he worked from home. His condo was increasingly becoming more home to him than he thought it would. Winston-Salem was more home to him than he imagined it could be. And Juliette wouldn't leave his thoughts.

He sat on his balcony at night and watched the lightening bugs flying around aimlessly, looking for trouble. He thought blonde thoughts. He dreamed of eternal smiles and long legs and beautiful eyes and a soul that seemed ageless, eastern and primeval. He thought of her. He couldn't help it. He contemplated the latest email from his grandfather,

"ALL THINGS EXCELLENT ARE AS DIFFICULT AS THEY ARE RARE."

On Sunday he went back to church and looked for Mrs. Carter. Her red hair shone like a beacon in a sea of gray. He asked if he could sit with her. She blushed. At least, she thought she blushed. It had been so long, she couldn't actually remember what blushing felt like. He asked how she was, she said, "I'm doing fine now Ahbinandan. I'm glad you came back for our worship service, or was it only me you came back for?" Now, it was his turn to blush.

He looked back at her and said, "My grandfather once told me that a man who chases two rabbits catches neither." She smiled, then paused as if to say something; then smiled again. They then shared a hymnal as they sang "The Old Rugged Cross." During the sermon, she slept and he reflected on the message: God promises us a safe landing, not a calm passage.

As they walked out of the church after the service, Mrs. Carter looked at him with a mischievous grin and said, "I'll bet your mother had her hands full with you." He smiled and replied, "My mother did indeed have a great deal of trouble with, but I think she enjoyed it." She looked up at him and said, "I'm sure she did. See you next week Abhinandan." He was already looking forward to it.

Chapter 18

MONDAY AFTERNOON HE WALKED DOWN THE STREET to Finnegan's Wake for some Irish stew and words of wisdom from his friend Opie. The stew was very good. On his return home he noticed a rather frail, skinny guy sitting on a bench outside his condo. As he started in the front door, the guy said something to him. Abbey wasn't sure what was said, so he looked at the guy and asked, "Can I help you with something?" The man said, "Yes, you can help me with something. Tell me where Juliette is and then get the crap out of her life!"

Abbey was shocked. How did this man know Juliette? And how does he know that I know Juliette? From his poker experience, he knew not to give away any information, so he said "I presume if Juliette wanted you to know where she was, she would've told you."

"Just tell me where she is Pedro before I beat the crap out of you."

He looked at Ian and said, "First of all, my name isn't Pedro. Secondly, I don't know who you are and even if I did, I wouldn't give you the time of day. Thirdly, take your best shot!"

Ian was a bully and a loudmouth, but he wasn't stupid. Abbey was at least 3" taller than him and probably thirty pounds heavier. As he took a step towards him, Ian turned to walk away and said over his shoulder, "You'll be hearing from me Jose. I'll get you." Abbey took two quick steps in his direction and Ian started running. He thought, "How does this skinny jerk know Juliette? And, how does he know me? And, why does he want me out of her life?" None of this made any sense to him.

He went up to his balcony and stared out towards Pilot Mountain, hoping it would render some thoughts of wisdom and explanation over this strange turn of events. But, as usual, the old knob of a mountain was silent. So, he typed out a quick message to his grandfather asking him his thoughts on human nature and how he reacted to people trying to push him around. After he finished a glass of Red Muscadine wine, the answer came back,

"SOMETIMES YOU HAVE TO BITE SOMEONE TO REMIND EVERYONE THAT YOU HAVE TEETH."

The problem was, he didn't know who to bite. He wished he'd followed this guy and learned something about him. He didn't know anything except that this jerk knew Juliette. And just like him, he also didn't know where she was. However, Ian knew who Abbey was. He had followed him and learned where he lived, where he worked and from Lonewolf's website, Ian now had Abbey's email address at work.

Usually, when Ian spouted off at someone, especially fellow dancers, they all cowered down to him and gave him what he wanted. He'd never had someone push back like Abbey had. Ian wasn't a fighter. He was bully and an intimidator. He went back to his apartment fuming at what had happened. He'd show Abbey he meant business. If he couldn't physically stand up to him, he'd bully him through cyber-space—so he thought.

94

Ian pulled up his video of the night he doped Juliette. He had deleted some of the video to show only short scenes of him groping her, of her with most of her clothes off and scenes where he had "posed" her provocatively lying in the bed. To someone unaware, it would seem to be a video of two lovers on the verge of an x-rated evening alone. This would be his revenge. He would send this to Abbey. He would now be back in control. Juliette and Abbey would now do what he ordered them to or risk this video becoming public.

Ian sent the video to Abbey with a text that read, "If you don't want this video to become public, tell me where Juliette is and then leave us alone FOREVER. Don't bother me or her again as long as you live. I am not playing."

Abbey received the video and could easily tell the guy in the pictures was the same skinny jerk who had confronted him. He could also easily identify Juliette. After the initial shock of seeing the video, he started thinking. He analytically reviewed each scene in regular time and in slow motion. In each scene he could tell Juliette was not really moving. She would be in one position, then the video would break and start back with her in a different position. He never actually saw her move in live motion.

He was also able to zoom in and could tell her eyes were almost shut, if not completely closed, in all the scenes. The videos never actually showed her doing anything. It showed Ian touching her. It showed Ian kissing various parts of her body. It showed Ian lying on top of her. But at no time did the video ever show Juliette responding or moving her arms and legs, or kissing Ian back. It was staged. He knew it. What he didn't know was how, or why, Ian had managed to do this. Certainly, Juliette would have never agreed to any of this nonsense. Did this have anything to do with her leaving?

He was thinking bad thoughts. Not about Juliette, but about Ian. He wanted to hurt him. He wanted to hurt him badly. Ian had no idea Abbey could trace him through his email. It took him about twenty minutes to find Ian's name, his address, what websites he visited, how much money he had in the bank, who his fifth grade teacher was and what he had for dinner last night. He was still thinking bad thoughts.

He needed to think. He needed to get away. He needed a distraction to get his mind off Ian and what he wanted to do to him. What better distraction than visiting his parents. If spending a weekend with them couldn't clear his mind, then nothing could. He loved his parents and would die for them. But, they could also worry him to death. A couple days with them was all he could handle before he went insane!

At their home, he was expected to wear traditional Indian clothing. All meals were traditional Indian cuisine—which he hated. The conversation was all things Indian and, of course, the everlasting question of why he wasn't dating any good Indian women? Maybe he would just spend one night with them.

His parents had planned a dinner party for his homecoming, which came as a surprise to him. Five others were invited. Four of them were professors at Appalachian State and the fifth guest was the daughter of one of the couples—also a doctor, with a PhD in Philosophy. Her name was Harpreet Chahal and she was a faculty member at Salem College in Winston-Salem.

Harpreet and Abbey both felt as though they were being set up. They were. Their parents had conspired and arranged the entire evening. Harpreet came dressed in traditional Indian attire. He wore a sport coat, button-down collared shirt, slacks and tasseled loafers. Harpreet handled the evening as pleasantly as she could. She made conversation and smiled when she should have, and laughed at all the American jokes (even though they weren't funny).

Unlike him, Harpreet was proud of her heritage, though she didn't want to be defined by it. She was an American citizen, but embraced her cultural roots. She had recently broken off a long affair with an Indian man because he wanted her to resign her position at Salem College and move with him to Washington D.C. where he was recently hired as a liaison officer at the Indian Embassy. She wasn't really sure if she truly loved this man or not, but she was sure he wouldn't be telling her what to do.

The evening unfolded uneventfully enough until Abbey made the mistake of comparing China's economy and potential to that of India's and the United States. This type of subject matter was not uncommon. Frivial matters such as family, sports, weather, vacations, or television were frowned upon by the intellectual snobbery of this dinner table.

When he suggested that China's potential was indeed staggering, Harpreet's father took it as a personal affront. He stood up from the dinner table and started his lecture— pointedly at Abbey. He said,

"I'll have you know sir, that the 25% of India's population with the highest IQ's is greater than the total population of the United States!" "I understand," said Abbey, "what I meant was…"

97

"And" her father continued, "India has more honor students in their schools than the United States has students!"

"What I meant to imply…" Abbey tried to say, but couldn't because her father continued….

"India is currently preparing students for jobs that don't even exist yet! While the United States is preparing their kids to be on reality TV shows."

At this point, Abbey decided discretion would be the better path to follow. He peeked a look at Harpreet and she whispered, "I tried to warn you."

Chapter 19

HE SPENT ONE NIGHT WITH HIS PARENTS and used work as an excuse to make the hour and a half drive back to Winston-Salem from Boone. His parents would never argue or interfere with work issues. Never. However, they did manage to slip him Harpreet's email address and phone number, along with several dishes of Indian food his mom had prepared for him to take home.

On the drive back through the Yadkin Valley Wine Region he thought of ways to physically hurt Ian. Certainly, he could do that, and he really wanted to. But, Ian still might send that video out which would hurt and embarrass Juliette. He couldn't take that chance. He knew exactly what he would do.

Back home in his computer room, he dissected the video from Ian. Then he made three videos of his own, inserting various new characters into the film. In the first video, Abbey had cut and pasted the face of Ian's mother onto Juliette's body. He found her picture on Ian's Facebook account. The second video cut out Juliette completely and showed Ian kissing and fondling a blow-up doll. The third video, which was his favorite, depicted Ian lying on top of a sheep, in a very romantic position.

He sent all three videos back to Ian and warned him if Ian tried to do anything with the original film, that he would anonymously send all three videos to Ian's Facebook friends, his employer, the School of the Arts and especially to Ian's mother. He didn't expect to ever hear from Ian again. But the bigger issue was, would he ever hear from Juliette again?

He had emailed his grandfather and told him about his trip to Boone and his parent's house. His parents visited India at least once a year, but didn't exactly see things the way Abbey's grandfather saw things. They didn't think his grandfather was "Indian enough." They thought that even though he had lived his entire life in India, he had let western culture and religion influence his life, and his grandson's life, too much. They knew of his influence on their son. They also knew there was little they could do about it.

His grandfather wrote back, "DID YOU ENJOY YOUR VISIT?"

"Yes, grandfather, your son is very predictable. He wants to be 'Indian' and he wants me to be 'Indian,' he just doesn't want us to live in India."

"WELL, AHBINANDAN, IT SEEMS AS THOUGH HE TREATS US BOTH THE SAME THEN. HE ALSO WANTS ME TO BE 'INDIAN.'

"Do you have any advice for me concerning your son?"

"ADVICE IS WHAT WE ASK FOR WHEN WE ALREADY KNOW THE ANSWER BUT WISH WE DIDN'T."

"That's very nice grandfather, but I need something more concrete."

"HERE'S MY ADVICE TO YOU CONCERNING YOUR FATHER... ALWAYS BE SINCERE, EVEN IF YOU DON'T MEAN IT."

Chapter 20

JULIETTE COULD TELL THINGS WEREN'T COMFORTABLE with her mom and dad. They were pleasant with her, but short and disinterested with each other. She knew there were unspoken issues—deep issues, which her parents chose not to discuss with her. And, she suspected there were serious disagreements between them when she wasn't around. They each seemed to have their own individual lives outside the home, that didn't include each other.

Her mom was involved in various charities and foundations and was always going to some meeting to either save the whales, or save the rain forest, or save the coast. Anything and everything except to save her marriage. Her dad had become a fulltime golfer after he retired. But he quickly discovered the nature of golf lent itself to frustration, irritation and disgruntlement. Playing good golf wasn't something that could be purchased—except with time and commitment. Her dad wasn't looking for that sort of investment.

He closeted his clubs and soon took up tennis at the local club, Revolution Tennis. He was still in fairly good shape and had always been a pretty good athlete, tennis suited him better. The club pro took a personal interest in him and spent many hours on individual lessons—on the court, and off.

Most tennis clubs had male pros, but not this one. They had a local woman who had grown up in Sausalito and had been a mid-level touring pro years ago. Her claim to fame was that she once took Chris Evert to three sets, before losing, at a tournament in Palm Springs. Back on those days, mid-level pros made very little money. The only endorsement deals were for the top women, everyone else had to scramble for what loose dollars were available. Thus, the teaching pro job at the local country club.

Rosie still had her tanned good looks (maybe a little wrinkled by the sun), her athletic body and a huge desire to snare a local rich guy to secure her future. She didn't want to be teaching forehands and backhands to little kids and old women her entire life. Juliette's dad seemed smitten by her and she did all she could to enhance his infatuation.

Rosie was not only athletic, but insatiable as well. She made Juliette's dad feel thirty years younger. He started exercising a little more, drinking a little less, cutting back on desserts and slightly coloring his hair. All in the vain attempt to fool himself into believing that he was indeed thirty years younger. He fooled no one, especially his wife.

She suspected something was going on. She didn't know who it was, nor particularly cared, as long as she continued to have access to her credit cards and all the bank accounts. She took Juliette shopping most days. She thought shopping and spending her husband's money would make Juliette feel as good as it made her feel. It didn't. Juliette could not forget Abbey. She couldn't forget how he made her feel. No amount of "stuff" could cure the feelings in her heart. She was thinking she had to get back to Winston-Salem soon and face the demons of Ian. She couldn't let this creep ruin maybe her only chance of happiness.

Juliette knew her parents were only being agreeable because she was there. She suspected the worst, but didn't know what to say to either of them. She loved her parents. Finally, she told her mom that she was going back home, to Winston-Salem. Her mother started crying, not because Juliette was leaving so much, but because she was losing her buffer between herself and her husband. She dreaded the thought of being in the same house with him alone again.

Juliette's parents accepted their daughter's decision to return to North Carolina. Her mom was sad. Of course, her dad seemed sad, but was still a little too titillated to feel much of anything, except the groping hands of Rosie. They planned a dinner for the three of them at the most exclusive restaurant in Tiburon that night. During the day, Juliette and her mom shopped and her dad had a tennis lesson he simply couldn't miss.

Juliette's mom went overboard shopping for her daughter, buying things Juliette didn't want or need. They were in the process of unloading the car at their home when her mom's cell phone rang. It was the hospital. They needed to get to the emergency room as soon as possible. Her husband had suffered a serious heart attack.

Her mom finished unloading all the packages from the car first, much to Juliette's dismay. By the time they arrived at the hospital, her husband had died. He had suffered a massive heart attack. There was no chance of reviving him. Juliette broke down in deep sobs and anguish. Her mom checked her watch and wondered if she should cancel the dinner reservations or not. The doctor came out and gave them the details as he knew them.

Her husband had been rushed to the hospital, unresponsive and with no discernible heart beat—and he was naked. Juliette's mom wanted to know where the ambulance had picked him up. The doctor made a call and found the address was 215 S. Cross Street. Juliette's mom pulled up the phone directory app from her smart phone. The first name she checked—no. The second name—no. The third name—yes. He was at the home address of Rosie Austin. She knew it had to be one of those three.

Funeral arrangements were made. Juliette's tickets to Winston-Salem were cancelled. She and her brother were distraught. Her mother went shopping. Juliette knew she'd have to stay a while longer now. She'd lost the most important man in her life, and she felt she was on the verge of probably losing the next most important man in her life. Her father left her too soon. She never had the chance to....

Now, she wondered if she'd lose that chance with Abbey as well.

Her mom asked Juliette to stay for awhile. She had no choice but to accept and help her mom through this period. Her mom played the part of the grieving widow to perfection. She accepted all the calls and visits between phone calls with her lawyer, who was tying up the loose ends of the huge life insurance policy and all the other financial details of her husband's death. The lawyer made sure everything was taken care of. Juliette's mom handled only one piece of business—personal business.

She personally called the country club and cancelled their membership. Then she called the tennis pro shop and spoke directly with Rosie Austin. She said, "I hope you enjoyed yourself with my husband. I want to personally thank you for teaching him the 'drop dead shot.' He finally learned to do something that made me happy." She smiled inwardly as she hung up the phone.

Juliette was in a quandary. She felt as though she needed to stay with her mom and brother for a while, but she wanted and needed to get back to Winston-Salem. She couldn't imagine what Abbey must be thinking right now. She left him with no explanation whatsoever. Maybe he didn't even care. But maybe he cared deeply—maybe he felt the same way she did. So many unanswered questions. She wanted to simply call him up and tell him the truth about everything. The entire wild, utterly useless truth. But she didn't.

Chapter 21

"YOU DON'T DROWN BY FALLING IN THE WATER, YOU DROWN BY STAYING THERE."

JUST AS HE ALMOST UNDERSTOOD this latest email from his grandfather, just before it all made sense—his thoughts on this lesson seemed to fade away like smoke through his fingers. He could feel it's meaning and sense it, but he couldn't grasp it.

He stopped by the art gallery again. Once again Martha told him the same stale story. She hadn't heard from Juliette and didn't know where she was. It was partly true. She really didn't know where Juliette was, but she had spoken with her on the phone several times. Still, she kept repeating the same lie to him. A few times, she even wondered if Abbey had given up on Juliette and was simply coming by to see her. A girl could dream.

Abbey focused on work. He'd been invited to a party given by the hospital staff, held at a local winery. Raffaldini Vineyards offered a fantastic view of the surrounding Blue Ridge Mountains and had a variety of dry and robust red wines. He wasn't a big fan of dry wines. However, he could tolerate the wine better than he could the dry, stale conversations at the party. The only consolation (aside from the view) was the appearance of Wendy Wasserman....Dr. Wendy Wasserman.

He had met her before at some meetings over at Baptist Hospital. When he discretely inquired about her, he was told she was divorced from a much older man, another doctor about 50 years old. It was clearly evident to Abbey that she would have better served by two men of 25. She was blonde, well-built, very intelligent and a few years older than him. Three out of four was not bad—not bad at all. Eventually, she made her way over to him and joined in the group conversation about billing rates, insurance gaffes and the high cost of medical malpractice premiums.

He tried nodding and smiling at this meaningless, trivial conversation. He truly thought these magnificent minds would have found something more challenging and substantive to discuss than issues of money. He tried to unobtrusively drift away and try another wine that might suit him better, when someone touched him on the arm. Dr. Wasserman said, "It's so nice to see you here, I'm glad you could make it." She asked him how he liked the wine and Abbey replied, "The view is fantastic."

Dr. Wasserman said, "I really enjoy the Merlot. It has a deep, sensual taste that excites the imagination and leaves me with a nice, warm glow." Abbey, being Abbey, knew she wasn't referring to the wine. But even though she was blonde, beautiful and intelligent—she wasn't Juliette. Her smile didn't melt him, her legs didn't excite him, her presence didn't fulfill him. And really, who likes Merlot?

Probably for the first time in his life, he walked away from a beautiful, blonde woman. He walked toward the restroom, but slipped around the corner instead. He was in his car and on his way back towards his condo before Dr. Wasserman refilled her glass.

What was he going to do? He was at a dead end with Juliette. He hated to face the reality that she was simply avoiding him and wanted to be alone. Should he try to forget her and move on? Should he try to convince his heart it didn't feel the way it did? No. He had his reasons, which reason knows nothing about.

He went back to church Sunday because it made him feel good to hear the message and to see Mrs. Carter. She was in her usual spot, in the same pew she'd sat in for years and years. They sang some hymns together and she fell asleep during the sermon again. This time her head nodded over against his shoulder. He liked how it felt.

He knew very little else about Mrs. Carter, but she always seemed to be alone so he thought he'd ask her if she wanted to have lunch with him after church. As they walked outside after the service, he turned to her and said, "I'm thinking of having lunch here at the Salem Tavern, would you care to join me?" "Well Abhinandan, aren't you the rogue? Asking a married woman out on a date."

"I didn't know you were married," he replied, "I've never seen you with your husband before. I'm very sorry if I offended you."

"Oh hush," she said. "I am married, but I was just messing with you. My husband Paul is in a nursing home and I visit him each Sunday after church and tell him what the sermon was about."

He found this odd since she slept through all the sermons he'd been to. He wondered what she told her husband. He asked her, "It's nice you can do that. How long has he been in the nursing home?"

"Oh, I guess he's been there about a dozen years or so." And with the saddest expression he had ever seen, she continued, "He'll never leave there."

"I'm so sorry to hear that Mrs. Carter. It's very tough on everyone when a loved one is bed- ridden."

"Oh, he's not bed- ridden at all. He's all over that nursing home. He just doesn't know who he is, where he is, or who I am. He hasn't recognized me, or anyone for that matter, for several years."

"But you still go each Sunday to tell him about the sermon and talk to him?"

"Yes, I do. Even though he doesn't know me, I know him."

He hugged her....she hugged him back.

He became curious about Mrs. Carter's husband in the nursing home. He had no concept of the cost and charges for someone to be a patient in a total care facility. When he got home he looked online at the Arbor Ridges Care Facility and was totally surprised at the cost. Not that it was out of line with other facilities, but just the total cost itself—how did people afford

$6,000-9,000 a month? More specifically, how did Mrs. Carter afford it?

He started checking online. Mr. Carter had retired from RJ Reynolds Tobacco Co. and had a nice retirement plan and pension from them. Mrs. Carter had retired from the Winston-Salem/ Forsyth County school system, where she taught 6th grade for thirty-eight years. She too had a nice pension and retirement plan. But he knew that $9,000 a month would erode anyone's retirement plans very quickly.

He next looked online at several banks and finally found the bank Mrs. Carter used. He hacked (very easily) into their system and into Mrs. Carter's account and found that the joint account she has with her husband was down to less than $17,000 in total value. He went back through her history up to eight years ago (which was the farthest back the bank system had records for) and found that she and her husband had over $837,000 in their account eight years ago. Now, it was down to $17,000. Alzheimer's not only robbed people of their memories, it also robbed them of nearly everything.

He was dumbfounded. Mrs. Carter had enough for about two more months of care for her husband—then what? Sell her house? Declare bankruptcy? The cold hard facts of aging had never dawned on him as cruelly as this had. He checked online for Mrs. Carter's three children. One lived in Cary, N.C., another in Lumberton and the other in Jacksonville, N.C. All were retired. All had been teachers during their careers and were comfortable financially, but none was in a position to help their mom and dad. Teaching was an admirable profession, but not a lucrative one.

He had to think. He needed help. He wrote his grandfather and told him all about Mrs. Carter and her dilemma and asked for his advice. His computer was silent for too long. He started thinking he probably shouldn't have put this burden on his grandfather. After all, he was near the point of aging out as well and this entire scenario may have truly depressed him.

Finally, the message from India came through,

"ABHINANDAN, I KNOW YOU AS WELL, OR BETTER THAN YOU KNOW YOURSELF. I KNOW WHAT YOU CAN DO. I KNOW THE GOOD IN YOU. YOU CAN'T HELP EVERYONE, BUT YOU CAN HELP SOMEONE. NOT BEING ABLE TO DO EVERYTHING IS NO EXCUSE FOR NOT DOING EVERYTHING YOU CAN."

He knew what he had to do. And he knew how he was going to do it.

Chapter 22

JULIETTE'S MOTHER DIDN'T SEEM TOO AWFULLY distraught about her husband's sudden death. In fact, Juliette realized her mom was a little too happy when she thought no one was around. However, she continued to lay serious guilt feelings on Juliette to stay and "help" her through the grieving period. She constantly urged her to sell her "little shop" in Winston-Salem and move back home where she belonged. Her brother had gone back to school at Stanford and Juliette was feeling lonely. She missed her art gallery. She missed Martha and her friends. She missed her home in Ardmore. She missed Abbey and long talks by his fireplace. She missed his smile and his nature and his presence. She missed the way he made her feel.

Juliette didn't know what to do. How could she abandon her mother? Did Abbey have any of the same feelings she had? Had he forgotten about her? It was hard for her to face another dinner engagement, where her mother had invited an up-and-coming young man from the valley. They were all nice and charming, but they were all too Californian—if that makes sense. They were all trying to be interesting, trying to be sincere, trying to be funny and intelligent instead of just BEING.

Chapter 23

ABBEY DROVE BACK UP TO CHEROKEE and Harrah's Casino. He had a job to do. He had to make $9,000 this month to help Mrs. Carter's husband. He was confident in his poker skills and his ability to read people. He went directly to the "high stakes" room, where the minimum buy-in was $10,000. He bought $15,000 worth of chips and joined the table of five other players. He thought, "All I've got to do is ease into the action and get a 'read' on everyone before I get into the truly big money."

It didn't work out that way. The first hand he was dealt—the first hand—brought out all the action he needed. He was dealt an Ace and a "ten" which was a pretty good hand with five other players involved. The pot was raised and called and three of the other players folded their hands. He and two others now saw the flop of the three community cards. The flop came out Ace, Ace, ten. Oh, darling, Abbey now held a full house—three Aces and two tens.

The player to his left immediately announced that he was "all-in" and pushed his stack of over $21,000 into the pot. The next player folded and Abbey looked back at the first guy and asked him, "Did you say you were "all-in?" The guy looked back at him, smiled, and said, "You got it Senor."

He looked down at his two hold cards (the Ace and ten) just to make sure he didn't misread them and looked back at the other player and said, "I'm not Hispanic, and I call your bet." He pushed his whole stack of $15,000 worth of chips into the pot and turned over his cards. When the other player saw Abbey had Aces over tens, the smile quickly evaporated from his face.

The dealer asked him to turn his cards over. It really pained him to turn over the two tens he was holding. His two 10's, plus the flop of Ace, Ace, ten had given him a full house of three tens over two Aces—which was a great hand, but unfortunately for him, was not as good as Abbey's Aces over tens.

The dealer finished dealing out the last two inconsequential cards, then pushed the entire stack of chips over to Abbey—a little over $31,000. He collected his winnings, flipped the dealer a $100 chip, pushed his chair back and said as he was leaving, "The taxman is going to love me." In less than five minutes he had more than accomplished his goal. He now had over $16,000 in profit, which was nearly two months of care at Arbor Ridges for Mr. Carter.

He didn't really look forward to the long drive back to Winston that evening, so he called the Grove Park Inn in Asheville. They had a vacancy and he jumped at the chance to spend an evening at this luxurious resort. He drove over, checked in and then went out to the huge back porch and found a vacant rocking chair. He then ordered an Iron Maiden from the waiter and sat back to catch his breath and enjoy the magnificent view of the rolling Blue Ridge Mountains.

He pulled the laptop from his briefcase and sipped his drink while he emailed his grandfather. He wrote, " I hope you're well grandfather. I took your advice and did what I had to do."

After a few moments of introspection, the reply came back,

"BETTER TO LIVE ONE DAY AS A LION, THAN A THOUSAND YEARS AS A LAMB."

The Iron Maiden was tasting very good. He might have another one.

He had two pieces of business to complete. The first one would be easy. The second one might be more difficult—depending on how trusting Mrs. Carter was. First, he hacked into the bank account of Mrs. Carter, only to obtain her account number. Then, he went to his bank with his winnings and had a Bank Check made out to "Cash." Next, he went to Mrs. Carter's bank and deposited the Bank Check for $9,000 into her account. He knew that sometimes banks would question deposits over $10,000, so he decided to make all his deposits around $9,000.

Now, he had to hack into the Benefits Department of RJ Reynolds, the company where Mr. Carter worked and retired from. This took about eight minutes. He then wrote an email to Mrs. Carter, supposedly from the Benefits Department at RJ

Reynolds, telling her that her husband now qualified for "Extended Coverage" because he had reached the required age threshold. The email explained that RJR would start depositing around $9,000 each month into her account as part of her husband's extended coverage.

He found the name of some mid-level executive at Reynolds and signed his name to the email before he sent it. He could now only hope that Mrs. Carter didn't question this gift too much and try to call RJR to thank them. He simply wanted her to accept the money and let it be.

Waiting for church on Sunday was difficult for him. He really couldn't bring up the subject of the money, but he was extremely curious to find out what Mrs. Carter thought about her windfall. He walked up the steps to the church and looked down the aisle towards Mrs. Carter's usual seat and he saw her holding court with several men and women near her own age. She was very animated and excited as she waved her arms while she talked. He secretly hoped she was telling them all about her good fortune. And even more, he hoped none of the others were also RJR retirees who might call the Benefits Department wanting their special bonuses.

He waited for the crowd to clear from around her, which didn't happen until the organist starting playing "Amazing Grace." He then went down the aisle and took his seat next to her. She looked over at him, smiled and said, "Abhinandan, the Lord always looks after those who can't help themselves....don't ever forget that."

He smiled back and said, "I won't Mrs. Carter. Trust me, I won't." Then they all joined in the chorus,

"Amazing Grace, how sweet the sound,

That saved a wretch like me.

I once was lost, but now am found

Was blind, but now I see."

Chapter 24

AFTER THE CHURCH SERVICE, all Mrs. Carter's friends once again surrounded her, so he quietly slipped away and was walking down the sidewalk towards his car when someone called his name. He turned to look and didn't see anyone he recognized. In fact, there was only one person in the sea of gray that was looking at him. A quite attractive young lady, with long flowing dark hair, dressed in a conservative, yet sexy looking, pale blue dress and high heels was walking towards him.

She waved, but he had no idea who she was. He did know that she had a great tan, great legs and a marvelous body. She walked up to him said, "It's so great to see you again. How have you been?"

He could almost recognize the voice. Maybe it was someone from the hospital? Or, from some meeting he had attended?

She kept looking at him and said, "You don't know who I am do you?" Well, he could try to fake something, or could just admit the truth and tell her he didn't recognize her and apologize for the oversight. But before he could say anything, she said, "Harpreet, from the dinner at your parent's house."

He was absolutely stunned. Certainly, this couldn't be the same woman he'd met at his parent's house. That woman had her hair rolled up in a bun, was dressed in bulky, loose fitting Indian garments and was "Indian." This woman was sexy, very sexy, and not Indian! Was she?

She could tell he was having a hard time comprehending this entire sequence. So she told him, "I dress traditionally when I visit my parents. It means a lot to them. I've seen you here a few times, but didn't want to intrude on your visits with Mrs. Carter. She's such a nice lady."

He quickly regained his composure and replied, "I just wasn't expecting to see you here in church Harpreet. Are you a member?" "Yes, I am. My fiancée and I joined together about two years ago. The people are so loving and friendly here."

He then remembered she told everyone at the dinner that she had broken off the relationship with her fiancée because he wanted her to move to Washington, D.C. with him. He asked her, "Do you live near here?" She replied, "I do. I live downtown in a condo on 4th Street." He could hardly believe what she just told him. He said, "I live on 4th Street as well, in the Nissen Building. Where exactly do you live?"

"Well," she replied, "not in the Nissen Building. That would be a little too expensive for a lowly professor at Salem College." Before he could respond, a woman called out to Harpreet, asking if she was ready to go. She looked back at him and said, "My friend and I are going to lunch with her parents. Maybe we can get together sometime if you want to."

"Yes, that would be nice. Thanks for recognizing me Harpreet, it was good seeing you." She turned to walk back towards her friend and he could not move. There was something about an attractive woman in a nice dress, in high heels, who knew how to walk in those heels, that men simply could not ignore. And even though she wasn't blonde, he could not and did not ignore her walk.

He was still thinking about church and Mrs. Carter and his chance meeting with Harpreet when he got back home. He opened up his email and quickly wrote to his grandfather, "I went to church again today. I feel as though things are truly getting better, I think God might really love me." In a few minutes, the reply came through,

"ABHINANDAN, GOD LOVES YOU BECAUSE OF WHO GOD IS, NOT BECAUSE OF ANYTHING YOU DID OR DIDN'T DO."

At lunch, Harpreet's friend, Dianna, asked her who the good-looking guy was she saw her talking to at church. "Oh, he's just a family friend who recently moved here. I don't really know him." Dianna said, "Well, I'd like to know him! Do you think you could introduce me to him?" Dianna's dad asked, "Who are you talking about? I thought you were dating Brent." "Well, I am sort of dating Brent, but you know we're not serious. We just hang out and have fun."

Her dad said, "Well, I like Brent. He seems like a nice young man and he has a great job." Dianna had heard all this before, "Okay dad, then leave mom and you marry Brent." "You know what I mean," he said. "Who is this friend of Harpreet's you want to meet so bad?" Harpreet told them his name Abhinandan and he was a friend of her family and that she had only met him once in her life.

"Abhinandan?" Her mother asked. What sort of name is that? "He's Indian," replied Harpreet, "just like me." Dianna, her mother and her father all stopped eating and stared at Harpreet. Finally, Dianna said, "You're Indian?" "Yes," Harpreet answered, " I am. I thought you knew."

Dianna's mother finally spoke and said, "American Indian or India Indian?" It was all Harpreet could do to keep from laughing out loud. She had been friends with Dianna for over two years now and this subject had never come up. "My family came from India, I was born here in North Carolina and I'm an American citizen—as are my parents now."

Her mother said, "But you don't look Indian." Dianna chimed in, "I always wondered how you kept your tan all winter long." Harpreet looked back and said, "Well, now you know." Her dad started on his dessert and said, "I always liked Ravi Shankar." Without any pause at all, Harpreet replied, "Really? I'm a big George Strait fan myself."

After a few moments of awkward silence, Dianna said, "Well, I don't care what you are Harpy, or what he is. I still want to meet him." Harpreet smiled and ate a spoonful of crusted topped apple cobbler with ice cream. Dianna was her closest friend in Winston-Salem, but friendships have their limits.

Chapter 25

HE DECIDED TO MAKE HIS WEEKLY VISIT to the art gallery and talk with Martha again, and again hear her same old story. On his walk down, he started thinking about Martha. He was certain she knew more than she was telling him. He was also fairly certain that somehow Ian was involved in this entire mess. Finally, he was entirely certain he could bluff Martha and she would then spill everything she knows. In fact, he knew this would work. Martha loved to talk and he was sure, if given the right opportunity, she would tell him everything from her first kiss in junior high school, to what she ate for breakfast this morning.

He walked in the gallery and Martha was sipping hot tea while reading a novel called "The Red Storm" by a local Winston-Salem author, David Lusk. She looked up and Abbey said, "Oh Martha, thank God you're here. I just got off the phone with Juliette and she's so upset with this whole Ian thing. I don't know what she's going to do."

Martha almost spilled her tea and said, "You don't think she's going to close the store do you?" Abbey continued, "I don't know. She really can't take too much more of the drama. Between Ian, the store and you, I think she's about to do something drastic."

"Me? I've done everything she told me to do. She shouldn't blame me on her problems with Ian. I told her he was trouble but she wouldn't listen to me. I can't afford to lose my job just because that crazy Ian won't leave her alone! I'm calling her right now."

"Just calm down Martha, let me call her for you and tell her none of this is your fault. She may get emotional on the phone with you, but she'll listen to me." "Okay," Martha said, "that's a good idea." He fumbled around in his coat as if he was looking for his phone, then said, "Oh great! I've left my phone in the office. Can I use your cell to call her? I'll get this whole thing straightened out in no time."

"Yes, here….please tell her I'm doing everything she wants me to and I haven't told Ian anything." He took the phone, looked at the number and memorized it. He then pretended to call, when actually he never hit "send." He waited a few seconds and said, "Juliette, how are you? I'm here at the gallery with Martha and everything looks great here." Martha smiled.

He continued, "Yes, she told me that. Uh huh, uh huh….yes, I'm sure Martha is doing everything you want her to. Oh no, I'm totally convinced you can trust her. Yes, I'll keep checking in with her. Okay, I'll tell her that. Alright, I'll talk to you later. Bye." Martha was bursting… "What did she say? Is she mad at me? When is she coming back? Is she keeping the shop open?"

"Martha, Martha, Martha….you worry too much. Juliette does indeed trust you and values your friendship greatly. She said to tell you everything is okay and to keep doing the great job you've done in her absence. And, whatever you do, don't tell that crazy Ian anything."

"Oh Abbey, thanks so much for helping me. You've made my day. I knew I could trust you, I never wanted to keep any secrets from you. I was just doing what Juliette asked me to." When Martha said that last sentence out loud, she paused as if to reflect on it's true meaning. Before she could react further, he said, " Martha my dear, thanks again, I'll be in touch. I need to get back to work now. Bye." And with that he rushed out the door leaving Martha deep in thought—or, deep in something.

Now that he had Juliette's number, what should he do with it? If she'd wanted to talk to him, wouldn't she have called him by now? Maybe it was both Ian and him she was trying to get away from. He was confused. He went to work. He had dinner at Finnegan's Wake. He spoke with Opie. He went to 6th and Vine and anywhere else where he could think. It didn't work. He still didn't know what to do. He finally emailed his grandfather telling him he was struggling with a great decision and didn't know what to do. The response came back,

"ABHINANDAN, THERE ARE THREE KINDS OF PEOPLE IN THE WORLD.

THOSE WHO MAKE THINGS HAPPEN.

THOSE WHO WATCH THINGS HAPPEN.

THOSE WHO DON'T KNOW WHAT HAPPENED.

WHICH ONE ARE YOU?"

He knew exactly which one he was. He had already hacked into the cell phone carriers database and knew where the phone calls from Juliette were coming from . All of them had originated from an address in Tiburon, California. The address in Tiburon's tax records was listed to Mr. and Mrs. Mark Gideon.

It was simple work for him to access Mark and Christine Gideon's tax records and history. They had a daughter, Juliette, and a son named Allen. They were also very wealthy. He didn't know why Juliette had changed her name from Gideon to McGranahan, but he knew for sure where she was now. He picked up the phone and called his travel agent, arranging airfare to San Francisco, and a rental car upon his arrival.

He took Friday off from work. The president was happy to give him anything to keep him happy. Lonewolf Enterprises had recently billed Novant Health the largest invoice in the history of their company because of work Abbey had done. If he hadn't been so preoccupied with Juliette and Mrs. Carter he could have (and should have) gone to the president and requested a raise. He would have received anything he asked for. Abbey wasn't concerned with money right now. He was concerned with love.

Chapter 26

HIS FLIGHT DIDN'T LEAVE UNTIL THE NEXT AFTERNOON. He planned this late flight so he would have time to drive back up to Cherokee for the night and visit the poker room again. His last visit had been very profitable. Playing cards would enable him to get everything else off his mind and hopefully get a little ahead on his payments for Mrs. Carter. He arrived at Harrah's around 9:00 PM and went straight to the high stakes poker room.

A few of the same players were at the table, along with some new guys he didn't know. It would take him awhile to figure everyone out and get the "reads" he needed. He started out slowly, unlike his last visit, he did not get any monster hands to take advantage of. In fact, after nearly three hours of playing he hadn't had any good hands at all.

He thought he knew the tendencies of each player however, but he just couldn't get a hand which he could take advantage of. He noticed that one of the players, a guy who said he was from Atlanta, was either having very good cards dealt to him, or else he was an excellent bluffer. Abbey thought the latter. Nearing 1:00 AM, he was only up about $275, which wasn't much considering the buy-in at this table was $15,000. Sometimes, no matter how good you are and how well your reads are, the cards simply aren't kind to you. He was having that kind of night.

He didn't want to spend the night at the casino, so he had to decide whether to take a chance at a large pot, or just call it a night and try to win his $9,000 next week. Again, he was dealt a mediocre hand, a seven and eight of clubs. He was a sucker for these type of suited connector hands, where you had the possibility of either a straight or a flush.

The hand was raised and all the other players folded except him, a woman named Michelle and the guy from Atlanta named Lance. Abbey wanted to see the flop, hoping he would get lucky. He didn't. The flop had one Ace, one ten and one four—two of which were clubs. He missed his straight, but now he had four clubs and only needed one more club dealt to him to make a flush, which would probably win him the pot.

Lance bet $2,000, Michelle called that bet as did Abbey— hoping a club would be dealt next. It wasn't. A King of diamonds came out. The pot was now nearly $10,000 and Lance bet another $3,000. Michelle quickly folded and he started thinking. He had less than a 17% chance that the last card dealt to him would be a club. Was he willing to take that chance for another $3,000?

He was feeling lucky. He didn't know why, but he was. He was pretty sure Lance didn't really have a monster hand. He felt Lance had something small and was also hoping to push everyone else out of the hand by making a large bet. Abbey called the bet, increasing the pot size to over $16,000. The last card was dealt—a six of hearts—which broke his heart. He missed out on his flush and now had absolutely nothing.

Lance stared at him. He stared back. Lance bet another $3,000. Abbey really only had two options now: fold, as any sane person would do, since he had no hand whatsoever, or bluff and raise the pot hoping Lance would fold. He was pretty sure Lance had a pair. Maybe a pair of Aces, or more probably, a pair of tens—something small like that.

He had to trust his "reading" skills now, because he was going to bluff. Abbey said, "I call the $3,000 and raise all-in." Which meant he pushed all his nearly $16,000 worth of chips into the middle. He was betting almost $16,000 with nothing!

Lance stared at him longer. He stared back. Lance was trying to get a "read" off him. He already knew Lance. Just as it seemed as though Lance was thinking of calling his all-in bet, Abbey thought of something. He was still looking at Lance and said, "A man's gotta know his limitations."

He had heard Clint Eastwood say this in a movie to some punk he was about face down. He thought it appropriate to use at the time. He hoped it would work. He REALLY hoped it would work.

After two more minutes of intense staring from each player, Lance folded his cards. Abbey had just won a pot of nearly $18,000 with NOTHING! He gathered all his chips, flipped the dealer a $100 chip and went to cash in his winnings. It was late, but adrenaline would keep him awake on the drive back to Winston that night.

He slept a few hours before he had to leave and catch his flight to San Francisco. He tied up a few loose ends at work and opened the latest email from his grandfather. He hadn't mentioned going to California, nor much of anything else to his grandfather. Certainly, he said nothing about the last several weeks with the mystery surrounding Juliette. However, he knew that somehow his grandfather could apparently sense things that were happening in his life. He never understood this cosmic perception. He opened the email and it read,

"JUST BECAUSE THE PAST DIDN'T TURN OUT LIKE YOU WANTED IT TO, DOESN'T MEAN YOUR FUTURE CAN'T BE BETTER THAN YOU EVER IMAGINED."

He didn't really know what his future would be like. He did know that he'd like to explore the possibility of Juliette being a part of it—a big part of it. He finished packing and was ready to walk out the door when he received a text message. He didn't recognize the number, but the message read,

"Abbey, hope I'm not bothering you. There is a traditional blue grass recital at Salem College tonight. Was wondering if you'd be interested in going with me? Harpreet."

He had to read this a couple of times to fully comprehend the message. Harpreet is asking me out on a date. Right? Or, is she just being friendly? Are her parents forcing her to make the effort to keep family friendships in force? He was confused. He typed back,

"Thx so much, but I'm just leaving on a business trip. Be gone for a few days, I'll text U when I return." Well, that was sort of the truth. He thought it was okay.

"Ok, C U then" That was all. Should he reply to that? He wasn't sure of the protocol here. Anyway, he had to go. He tried to not think about the text on the drive to Charlotte, where he'd catch the non-stop flight to San Francisco. "Ok, C U then." He wasn't sure what the text meant. He kept trying to block it from his mind. There were too many other things occupying his thoughts now. He drove all the way to the airport exit in Charlotte trying consciously not to think of the message, but being totally unable to forget it… "Ok, C U then."

Chapter 27

HE FOUND THE RENTAL CAR AGENCY and somehow made his way out of the airport traffic mess and headed north. He tried to skirt the city, but traffic was congested and heavy in all directions. He finally crossed over the Golden Gate Bridge, but couldn't see the top of it because the fog was so thick. He drove up US 1 through Sausalito, Marin City and around Richardson Bay to the small town of Tiburon, which overlooks Angel Island out in the San Francisco Bay. Juliette's parents paid a hefty price for this view.

He had their address programmed in the GPS and it led him to a gated community with a guard sitting inside a small office, where he was watching television. He pulled up and told the guard he was here to visit the Gideons. The guard said, "Oh, I was so sorry to hear about Mr. Gideon's passing. I hope the family is coping okay. Are they expecting you?" Abbey didn't know anything about Mr. Gideon's death, but he quickly responded, "Yes, I'm here to help them with the estate and taxes and wills. You know how those things are."

The guard had no clue how those things were, but he let him pass with no further questions. Their house was on a street with an ocean view, called Moonlight Bay. It wasn't directly on the ocean, but still had a very nice view—a very expensive view. As he pulled into the driveway he suddenly realized he had no plan whatsoever. He'd spent all his energy and time and thoughts on getting here and finding Juliette's house. Now that he was here he went completely blank.

Since he had no plan, he decided to just walk up to the front door and ring the bell. If Juliette didn't want to see him, he would simply turn around and leave. But if she did.....well, he was hoping for this option. As he started up the door steps, the elaborately decorated mahogany front door opened and an elegantly dressed woman, holding a wine glass, stood looking at him. "I've already called the authorities." She said, "They should be here in about thirty seconds."

"I didn't mean to startle you ma'am, I'm a friend of Juliette's from North Carolina. I was out here on business and thought I'd drop by to see her." He continued his lies. "I'm sure if you tell her Abhinandan is here, everything will be okay."

"No, it won't be okay Mr. Abhinandan. Juliette is not here. She is out shopping for a wedding dress for her marriage in a few months." Just then, a different security guard drove up with his lights flashing. "Is everything okay Mrs. Gideon?" "Yes," she said, "this young man was just leaving." She looked at Abbey and continued, "Isn't that right Mr. Abhinandan?" He was almost too stunned to respond. Wedding dress? Marriage? "Yes ma'am, I'm leaving. Please tell Juliette I dropped by. I'm sorry if I frightened you."

He got in his car and drove away, with the security guard following him through the exit gate. He drove a couple of blocks to an overlook of the ocean and pulled off the road. He wasn't interested in the view. He couldn't believe what he'd just heard. Marriage? Wedding dress? His world was upside down. He suddenly realized that he was indeed in love with

Juliette and now it was all lost. The first woman he'd ever been in love with was gone.

Finally, a city policeman pulled up behind him, got out and walked up to his car. "Are you okay sir?" Abbey looked up at him and said, "I thought I was officer, but I was mistaken. Sorry to have bothered you, I'll be on my way." He drove aimlessly. Just driving to be driving. Going nowhere. He ended up back in Sausalito and saw a sign for "Scenic View" and took the long and winding road up to the top of a bluff where it overlooked the Golden Gate Bridge, with San Francisco in the background.

He sat there until almost dark when another police car came up to him and the officer said the park was closing and all visitors had to leave. He didn't know he was in a park, but he left. His first day in California and he'd already had three officers confront him. He found a small bed-and-breakfast on the backstreets and checked in for the night. It would be a long night. Wedding dresses and marriage. It would be a long night indeed.

At least he now understood why Juliette left so suddenly. She was in love. But he didn't understand anything else. "I should've known better," he thought. He had little choice now but to go back home, try to forget Juliette and get on with his life. It was going to be a long flight home.

Juliette came back home from her hair appointment to find her mother having a mimosa, which wasn't that unusual. Her mother said, "I need you to go through all your father's papers and personal items to see which ones you want to keep or give to your brother." Juliette said, "No, you look through everything first and keep what you want before we look at it."

Her mother took another sip of mimosa and replied, "I don't want any of it. You and your brother take what you want and throw the rest of it away." With that, she turned and walked towards the bar. Her drink needed refreshing.

Abbey logged into the airport's wifi network to check his emails. He returned some inquiries from work and deleted all the other assorted jokes and junk. He checked his investment portfolio, but really wasn't interested in financial affairs, not when his heart was broken.

He had two unopened emails from his grandfather. He did read those.

"THINGS WILL HAPPEN. YOU CAN'T STOP THEM FROM HAPPENING, BUT YOU CAN CONTROL YOUR REACTION FROM MAKING THINGS WORSE. REACT POSITIVELY. LIVE HAPPILY."

And,

"YOU ARE WHAT YOU DO, AND WHAT YOU DO... IS UP TO YOU."

Chapter 28

HE GOT BACK HOME LATE, which didn't really matter, he couldn't sleep anyway. He dozed a bit, but grew restless and finally got up and drank coffee. He loved his Keurig and a toasted bagel early in the morning. He was glad it was Sunday morning. He was looking forward to the comfort of church and the company of Mrs. Carter again.

He walked up the steps of the church and entered the foyer where he stopped to look for Mrs. Carter, who was usually very easy to spot. However, he didn't see anything bright and red in her pew. He looked around and didn't see her anywhere. An usher asked him if he needed any help and Abbey said, "Yes, I was looking for Mrs. Carter, but I don't see her."

The usher said, "Oh, I'm sorry, but she's gone." He felt as though he was paralyzed. Gone? He knew she was old, but she seemed to be in great health. This was indeed one of the worst weekends of his life. First Juliette gone and now Mrs. Carter. He looked back at the usher and asked, "What happened? I didn't know she was ill."

The usher looked puzzled and finally said, "Oh, no. She's fine. She's just gone for the weekend visiting her son. She should be back next week." Abbey exhaled with relief, but at the same time he wanted to just scream. Instead, he sat next to her empty seat and sang "What A Friend We Have In Jesus," and listened to the sermon concerning temptation, forgiveness and redemption.

During the church service, he looked around the sanctuary but didn't notice Harpreet anywhere. He wasn't sure if he was disappointed or relieved. He also wasn't sure how he felt about Harpreet. All his thoughts lately had been on Juliette. He still couldn't stop thinking about her. Even now, when he knew she was marrying someone else, he couldn't get her out of his mind. He didn't think he'd ever be able to.

After church, he went over to Hanes Park and found a secluded tennis court, rented a ball machine and hit tennis balls until he nearly broke a sweat. As he was hitting backhands a thought flashed in his mind. If the program he designed for Baptist Hospital enhancing medical imaging worked as well as they said it did, then why couldn't that same concept be used elsewhere? He'd look into that Monday morning.

One of the effects of having a mind like his was that he couldn't simply "turn it off." His brain kept thinking and wondering why and how and if. He was now getting too near the perspiration point. He needed to stop hitting balls. He needed a diversion. He'd seen an ad in the paper about a new winery opening up on the eastern end of 4th Street, near the Innovation Sector. He couldn't remember the name of it but he knew about where it was.

It was easy to locate but hard to find a parking space. The "Sun King Winery," was obviously very popular, probably because it specialized solely in wines from the Yadkin Valley wine district of North Carolina. He eventually made his way into the winery and found a small table outside and was looking over the wine list, searching for something sweet—but not too sweet. The waitress came over and asked him if he was ready to order yet. He looked up and realized it was Annie Norwood, the young mother who begged him for help that day protesting at the hospital.

She didn't seem to recognize him in his tennis outfit, so he didn't bring up the day of the protests and picket lines. He hoped she and her son were doing well though. He ordered a "blend" of three white wines, promising a "flavorful aroma, sure to challenge and satisfy the most discerning of palettes."

The order came with an assortment of cheeses and small crackers as well as the wine. It was all wonderful. The wine could have had just a tiny bit more residual sugar for his taste, but still, he enjoyed it. Annie Norwood was very busy. The place was full of the yuppie, mid-level, debutante, my-daddy-is-important crowd. There were several attractive, young ladies, with and without gentleman companions, at the other tables. He looked, but was only interested in the wine and cheese—and thoughts of Juliette. How long was this going to last?

He ordered a second glass and watched as the table of eight next to him all stood up and gathered their purses, i-phones, scarves, sunglasses, i-pads, i-pods and BMW key chains. One young man, with the whitest teeth and shiniest fingernails, handed Annie Norwood the payment and they all left laughing and looking around to see who was looking back at them.

Annie waited until they were gone, then looked at the payment and disgustedly murmered "Assholes." She didn't think anyone heard her little missive, but Abbey was paying attention and knew they had stiffed her on the tip. He finished his second glass and asked Annie for the bill. She was as pleasant and professional as she could be. She had every right to be bitter, but she kept it to herself.

He usually paid by credit card, but not this time. He pulled out two $100 bills, wrapped a $20 bill around them and left it under his wine glass as he walked out. He now had two cases to anonymously contribute to. It made him feel good. It made him temporarily forget thoughts of Juliette. Only temporarily however.

He went back to his condo, waited till dusk, then lit a fire and sat out on the deck watching the flames. He didn't hear the crickets, nor did he notice the owls calling for dinner. He stared at the embers, watching the flickering fire—the color reminding him of blonde things. How long would it take for his mind to release these thoughts?

He called his parents, just to get his mind on something else. The same answers to the same questions each week: "Yes, I'm eating well. Yes, work is good. I'll get my hair trimmed next week (Not). I'm not sure when I'll get back up there…it's very busy at work." Then, something new, his mother said, "Have you called Harpreet yet?" He stumbled a bit, not knowing exactly how to answer this. He didn't want them to know he'd met her at church. He didn't want them to know anything.

"No, not yet. As soon as work slows down, I'll contact her." He could always use "work" as the ultimate excuse for everything with his parents. "Yes, tell dad I love him too. No, I haven't heard from grandfather lately." (He lied again). "Okay mother, I need to go start on this paper for work now. I'll call you soon. I love you. Goodbye." And, he did love his parents. It just drove him crazy talking to them.

A momentary feeling of melancholia surged over him. He couldn't release his feelings about Juliette. He emailed his grandfather and asked the age old question that each and every human in the history of the world has asked themselves at one time or another: "Grandfather, do you think I'll ever find love—true love?"

He wasn't sure he wanted to know the answer to this question. He trusted his grandfather, his grandfather knew him inside and out. What if his grandfather saw something in him that he knew would prevent him from ever being happy and finding true love? He wished he hadn't sent that email now. He turned his computer off and stared at the fire.

He thought, "I wish I'd never met Juliette! She's ruined me." Then he thought, "Are you crazy? She was the most alluring, most beautiful, most enchanting woman I've ever been around. Having her in my life for one day was worth a lifetime of loneliness." After the fire eventually died out, he went to bed. He didn't sleep. Why? Because, tomorrow never knows.

At first light, he rose and turned his computer on. He didn't care about his Keurig or bagels—he cared about the response from his grandfather. The message was there. He hesitated a few moments before opening it. How would he answer the question of if I'll ever find love? The message read,

"YES, ABHINANDAN, YOU WILL. TRUST ME! I HAVE FOUND THAT IF YOU LOVE LIFE, LIFE WILL LOVE YOU BACK."

Chapter 29

HE WAS MISERABLE AT WORK THAT WEEK. He couldn't stop thinking about those two cruel phrases Mrs. Gideon spoke of: wedding dresses and marriage. He stopped going by the art gallery. He didn't want to face Martha, just in case she figured out the ruse he played on her, or if she knew of Juliette's wedding. He couldn't have stood that if she started talking about it. So he stayed away.

He started to text Harpreet, but decided against it. He was lonely, but he wasn't lonely for Harpreet. He was just lonely and it wouldn't be fair to her. He went to Finnegan's Wake after work and spoke with his friend Opie, whose silly jokes always seemed to cheer him up. It didn't this time.

He went to a movie by himself one night. He worked late (even though there was no need). He tried new restaurants—anything to divert his attention. It didn't work. Saturday morning, he walked down the street to Camino's Bakery and ordered a pastry and coffee and sat outside watching the traffic pass by. It was a great place to do some people watching because of all the apartments downtown and Gold's Gym being across the street.

There was always lots of pedestrian traffic Saturday morning. There were lovers walking down the street holding hands.

There were overweight people trying to burn off the calories from last night's pizza and beer. There were always dozens of young people with tattoos on every inch of their skin, strolling around showing off their "ink." And, there were joggers running aimlessly up and down the street trying to either impress themselves or everyone else. He was unsure which.

He just started his second cup of coffee and noticed a single young lady in running shorts and tank top jogging down the street towards him. "Wow," he thought, "she has nice legs. Really nice legs!" He tried to appear to be drinking his coffee, when he was actually positioning himself for a better look at her legs as she approached. When she had jogged almost up to his table, she suddenly stopped and said, "Abbey? What a surprise! You're not stalking me are you?"

He almost spilled his coffee all over himself as he looked up and realized it was Harpreet. He stammered, "Umm, no, I was just…I was having coffee." She smiled at him and said, "Well it seemed to me like you were staring at my legs."

Juliette may have left him speechless, but not other women. He rose and said, "Actually I was, I noticed you had a slight crowfoot in your stride and I was wondering if it caused you any pain as you ran." Before she could answer that unanswerable statement, he said, "Would you care to take a break and join me for coffee? I'm sure your feet would appreciate the rest."

She arched her eyebrow, looked down at his half-eaten pastry, then smiled as she replied, "I appreciate the offer, but one of us has to maintain a healthy diet and slim figure to ensure the public's perception of the ideal Indian persona." Before he could think of a reply, she was off and running. His only consolation was that the view of her running away was better than the view before.

He was looking forward to church on Sunday morning. He was hoping Mrs. Carter was back and he was subconsciously hoping Harpreet would be there as well. Mrs. Carter was easy to spot, her hair had been recently touched up and was now a lighter shade of red—almost orange. But somehow, it worked for her. She had saved him a seat next to her and as he sat down she looked over at him, smiled and said, "I hope you're feeling well today Abhinandan."

He smiled back and replied, "I am now Mrs. Carter." He thought she might have blushed, but it was hard to tell through the layers of makeup. After the hymns were sung and the offering taken, she once again fell asleep with her head resting on his shoulder. He enjoyed the feeling.

He looked around the sanctuary during the sermon and closing hymn but didn't see Harpreet. He was still unsure if he was disappointed or relieved. After church as they were walking out, he asked Mrs. Carter how her husband was doing, but before she could answer Harpreet suddenly appeared from behind and spoke to Mrs. Carter saying, "Good morning Mrs. Carter, I hope you're well. It seems you have a gentleman friend with you today."

Mrs. Carter looked at them both and replied, "He knows I'm taken. But if he'd been around about seventy years ago, things might be different now." Everyone laughed, except Mrs.

Carter. She was deadly serious. She saw a group from her Sunday School class and wandered over to them, leaving Harpreet and Abbey alone. He said, "Good to see you again Harpreet, I didn't know you were here this morning."

She smiled and said, "I saw you looking around for me during church. I was sitting in the balcony today." He quickly replied, "I wasn't looking around for you, I was looking for Mrs. Carter."

"You were already sitting next to Mrs. Carter. You were looking for me alright. I have some friends waiting for me outside. I'll see you later."

Before he could respond, she walked away. Twice now, she'd gotten the best of him. But again, his consolation was that the view of her walking away was well worth it. He thought to himself, "There's no way that's an Indian woman. I've never seen an Indian woman act like that, or walk like that!"

Harpreet's friend Dianna was waiting for her outside the church. As they met and started walking towards their car, Dianna asked, "Well, did you tell him I wanted to meet him?" "No, I didn't. He's not your type."

"Tall, dark, handsome and rich is not my type? Are you crazy girl? Get back in there and tell him you have a gorgeous friend who wants to meet him."

"Oh hush, you're acting like a teenager."

"Okay, I get it now. You want to keep him for yourself don't you Harpy?"

"Don't be silly Dianna. I have no interest in him at all, and neither should you."

"And, pray tell, why not?"

"Because he's old-time Indian, Dianna. All Indian men expect their women to serve them at all times. To be obedient to their wishes, do whatever they say and never question anything. Is that what you want?"

Dianna frowned, then squinted, then puckered her lips and finally said, "With him….YES."

"Well, then you're an idiot! I would never let a man treat me like that."

"I bet your dad doesn't treat your mom like that. In fact, from what I hear, she's the boss of your house."

"Just hush and get in the car. He's not for you and that's that!"

"Okay, okay…just calm down."

"I am calm. You just don't understand the Indian way Dianna."

"I'll tell you what I do understand……Harpy's got a boyfriend!"

"OH SHUT UP!!!!"

Chapter 30

LONEWOLF ASKED ABBEY IF WOULD LEAD a national seminar on their latest innovations (all of which came from his mind) being held in Las Vegas. There would be representatives from every major medical group in the country, as well as technicians from Google, Microsoft, Apple, Hewlett- Packard and many other smaller, yet more aggressive companies. All eager to hear what he had done and what he was planning on doing. And more importantly, what they could possible steal from him for themselves.

The President of Lonewolf lived in constant fear that one of the "big boys" was going to make Abbey an offer he couldn't refuse. Therefore, he treated him like royalty on this trip to Vegas, he wanted the best for his prize employee. While he couldn't get the Presidential Suite at Bellagio, he did reserve the next best one available. That wasn't all. Abbey had a personal valet for his four day, three night stay and Lonewolf had deposited a line of credit for him in the casino for $25,000.

As usual, he wowed all the attendees with ideas and concepts they'd never dreamed of. However, he and the President decided they certainly would not divulge any future plans they had. They would keep Abbey's ideas and handiwork to themselves for future profits. The meetings and seminars and demands on his time kept him busy all day and he loved it.

Especially the time with representatives from Microsoft, Apple and H-P, where they all pushed each other for ideas, while covertly trying to pillage, pilfer and pinch anything they could from each other.

After the meetings and dinners, where he was the star attraction, a bevy of beauties was always around offering drinks, companionship and whatever else might be on the minds of a bunch of geeks and nerds away from their wives for a week. He wasn't interested. However, he was interested in the casino, especially the poker rooms.

At Harrah's in Cherokee, the high stakes poker room had a buy-in of $15,000. Here in Vegas, high stakes meant million dollar pots. Abbey was confident in himself, but not that confident, and certainly not reckless. He would stick to the lower level tables where he would use the $25,000 Lonewolf had set aside for him.

His first night there he sat at a table where he was the only American. Every other player was speaking a foreign language and he couldn't tell what most of the languages were. What he did understand, very quickly, was that these guys were ultra aggressive and very bold. None of them liked to fold a hand, and each of them tried to win pots by out-betting their opponents.

It seemed to him that it really didn't matter who had the best hand. It mattered more who made the biggest bet. It was a game of testosterone-fueled, macho-inspired, who had the biggest cojones bluffing. He lost over $11,000 in the first half hour. Roy, we're not in Kansas anymore!

He had to change his approach. He had to stop playing the cards and start playing the men. He tried his best to lay low and familiarize himself with each player's tendencies and actions. He lost another $6,000 doing this. He was now down over $17,000 in the first two hours of a three-night stay.

He made a slight comeback the rest of the night by trying to stay away from the big pots and studying each of the players. He decided to call it an evening at midnight. He had a 9:00 AM seminar in the morning and wanted to get some sleep. He cut his losses to just over $7,300 for the session, which was quite a comeback from being down over $17,000 at one point.

The next day's meetings were all about other companies probing Abbey for information, trying to get him to divulge what he was working on. Good luck with that. One of his competitors, he never knew who, had a beautiful blonde woman in her late 20's start hanging around him all day. She did a great job of pretending to be a computer technician from an unknown Silicon Valley start up company. She hung on his every word, laughed at anything humorous and volunteered to bring him drinks and snacks throughout the day.

A couple of times she "inadvertently" brushed up against him during meetings. And once sat directly across from him at a small group conference and did her best Sharon Stone leg crossing imitation. If she hadn't been SO blatant about her intentions, he may have taken the bait. But it was clear to him that someone was trying everything underhanded they could to get close to him, or compromise him in some way.

However, and he couldn't explain this, he was still not over Juliette. For the first time in his life he wasn't interested. Well, he was interested. But the woman he was interested in was trying on wedding dresses in California. Or, so he thought. Still, he couldn't help how he felt. His heart still melted at the thought of her. His consciousness could not release the memory of that smile, or the contours of her legs and body. The hook was in deep and he didn't know how to release it. Heck, he didn't know if he wanted to release it.

At the end of the day, the young blonde came next to him and said, "I'm here alone tonight. Would you like to join me for dinner? I have reservations at 8:00." He smiled at her and replied, "I really appreciate the offer, but I have other plans for the evening. You're a beautiful woman and I'm very flattered. Please tell your customer that it nearly worked."

She started to say something, but looked into his eyes and knew that he knew what was happening. She smiled back and said, "Maybe next time." He smiled and winked saying, "Maybe."

After a quick dinner at the best restaurant in the hotel, a place oddly enough named "Piggies," he took a quick shower, changed clothes and headed back to the casino. He found the table with most of the same foreign players from last night, which also included two new players. Judging from their accents, the two new guys were either from Australia or Great Britain. He took his seat and promptly folded the first eleven hands dealt to him.

He was building his memory bank, studying each player, observing when and how they folded and raised. After last night and early tonight, he felt he had good reads on the foreign players. One of the two English speaking guys was in way over his head. That much was easy to tell. The other guy was not.

Abbey finally had a decent hand, a pair of Jacks, and raised the pot up to $4,000. He knew at least one of the foreign guys would promptly call and raise him back, trying to push him out of the hand. They did. One guy double raised him up to $8,000 and the next guy raised it again to $12,000. It was very hard playing these men, each hand they tried to out-raise you hoping you would fold your cards.

He called all the bets and pushed his chips into the pot. Next came the three card flop. Ace, nine and four. He didn't figure any of the foreign guys had Aces, or they would have raised the pot even higher. Therefore, his pair of Jacks was probably the best hand. But still, he had $12,000 in the pot, so he just checked. The next foreign guy checked as well, but the other English speaking guy, a man with graying hair and a Fu Manchu mustache, raised another $5,000!

To call this bet would take nearly everything he had, but he figured he still had the best hand with the Jacks. He called the bet. The first foreign man folded, so it was just Abbey and Fu Manchu in the hand now with over $48,000 in the pot. The fourth card came and to his astonishment, it was another Jack, now giving him a set of three Jacks.

He checked his hand again, knowing Fu Manchu would bet; and he did, $10,000. Abbey didn't have $10,000 on him, but the casino had granted him a line of credit of $25,000 in addition to the $25,000 Lonewolf deposited for him. He asked the pit boss to access this money for him and then he quickly pushed his $10,000 into the middle.

For the first time all night, he saw Fu Manchu hesitate. They stared at each other for what seemed like an eternity. Each man glaring directly into the other man's eyes, soul and guts. Neither gave anything away. But Abbey knew that slight moment of hesitation was all he needed. He knew he had the best hand. He also knew Fu Manchu would try to push him out with a huge final bet. He was right.

The last card was dealt and it was another Ace. He saw Fu Manchu's eyes slightly dilate. He was wrong. Fu Manchu did have an Ace, and this last card now gave him three Aces—a nearly unbeatable hand. Except, that the last Ace dealt now gave Abbey a full house, his three Jacks, plus the two Aces.

Fu Manchu looked at him, then said something to the dealer, in a heavy brogue-ish accent, and the dealer looked at Abbey and said, "He wants to know how much more money you have." Abbey took a deep breath, smiled and remembered something his grandfather had always told him. He looked at Fu Manchu and said, "Without courage, all other virtues are useless." He pushed all his remaining $25,000 dollars the casino had credited him into the pot.

He could have sworn he saw a slight bit of perspiration on Fu Manchu's upper lip. But if he had three Aces, Abbey knew there was no way he was going to fold that hand. He didn't. He called the bet and they each turned over their cards. When Fu Manchu saw Abbey's hand he said, "Póg mo thóin!"

Wasn't that interesting? He could curse in something that was either Gaelic or Scottish. Abbey had won an enormous pot and he remembered a line from an old Kenny Rogers song, "You've got to know when to hold 'em, know when to fold 'em and know when to walk away." He knew when to walk away.

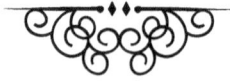

By the following day, the meetings had become repetitive and boring for him. He made an appearance and shook hands for awhile, but did not plan on staying there all day. He also did not see the young, attractive blonde woman anywhere. Apparently, her job was finished. Just before lunch, he slipped away. He had the concierge recommend a top notch tailor in town and he was going to put some of his winnings to good use.

Two blocks off Las Vegas Blvd the taxi dropped him off at Zimmerman and Son's. He stayed there nearly three hours picking out fabrics, styles and being fitted for four new suits, three pair of shoes (that would be handmade in London and shipped to him), six custom made shirts and seven silk and very expensive ties. This would be his only indulgence from his huge winnings.

He had already decided his last night in Vegas would not be spent at the high stakes poker tables. He loved playing, but did not really enjoy the tense atmosphere and huge stakes of the previous night—too stressful. He would play at tables with much smaller buy-ins and pots. He wanted to play for the challenge of reading his opponents, not to make money. He'd already done that.

He settled in nicely at a table with some cowboys, truckers and two salesmen from Dubuque, Iowa. He had them all figured out within fifteen minutes. He was up about $400 and having fun when someone tapped him on the shoulder. He looked up and a gentleman in a nice suit said, "Mr. Crean would like to invite you to come over and play at his table." He pointed across the way to the high stakes tables and Abbey saw Fu Manchu looking back at him.

So, his name is Mr. Crean. He looked back at the messenger and said, "Please tell Mr. Crean that I appreciate the offer and thank him for his hospitality and generosity last night. But, I'm staying here." He played a couple of more hours, winning a total of about $650 before calling it a night. He rode the elevator to the top floor and went inside the rooftop bar which overlooked "The Strip."

He ordered his favorite drink, an Iron Maiden, and let his mind start wandering. It didn't have to go far. Blonde thoughts immediately crept in and took over his consciousness. He thought of flying to San Francisco and driving over to Tiburon again with thoughts of trying to talk to Juliette and somehow win her back. But they were only dreams. He ordered a second Iron Maiden and convinced himself it was okay to dream. So he did.

Chapter 31

AFTER THE LONG FLIGHT HOME, he unpacked and read some emails. He had two unopened messages from his grandfather, whom he hadn't written since he left for Vegas. The first message read,

"IT IS FAR BETTER TO LIGHT A CANDLE THAN TO CURSE THE DARKNESS."

He had no idea what that meant. He often wondered if his grandfather sent him messages that were surreptitiously meant for himself and he was using Abbey as a conduit to his own consciousness. But, then again…maybe not.

The second message from his grandfather read,

"GROW EVERYDAY.

BE GRATEFUL.

BE RESPECTFUL.

BE OBEDIENT.

BE WISE."

He was trying.

He now had a little nest egg built up for his charity work. He wouldn't be so concerned with getting up to Cherokee EVERY week now. It was still a couple of weeks before he had to deposit another $9,000 in Mrs. Carter's account, but he wanted to go ahead and send Annie Norwood a small gift. He had a Cashier's Check from the bank made out to her for $1,100 and mailed it with no return address.

He made sure he was home from his trip in time for church on Sunday. When he arrived, Mrs. Carter was there in her usual place, waiting on him. After the usual pleasantries, she looked directly at him and asked, "I wasn't aware you knew Harpreet, are you two a couple?"

"Heavens no! I barely know her and she's definitely not my type Mrs. Carter."

"So, you don't like pretty women with good bodies Abhinandan?"

"That's not what I said Mrs. Carter."

"Well, what you say seems to differ from how you act."

"What do you mean by that?"

"Abhinandan, my friend, I saw how you were looking at her as she walked away from you last week. I think her bottom made quite an impression on you. Did it not?"

"Mrs. Carter! I can't believe you said that here in church."

"Well son, I may be a Christian alright, but I'm not dead."

As the choir started singing "Holy, Holy, Holy," Mrs. Carter could not hide her smile. She slept on his shoulder, as usual. He made a special effort not to look around the church, in case Harpreet was spying on him. After the service as he was walking Mrs. Carter down the aisle, once again, Harpreet came up behind them and spoke to Mrs. Carter.

"Good morning Mrs. Carter, you look lovely today. I hope you and your friend enjoyed the service."

"Oh, we did my dear. You should come and sit with us next time, I'm sure Abhinandan would enjoy your company. Wouldn't you Abhinandan?"

But before he could answer that loaded question, Harpreet said, "I'm not too sure of that Mrs. Carter, he seems perfectly happy being with you."

"Well my dear, that may be true, but I guarantee you he enjoys watching you walk much more than he does sitting with me."

Harpreet smiled and replied, "That's good to know, but I already suspected as much. Sorry I can't stay and chat but I must be walking away now. I hope you both have a wonderful day." She quickly turned and headed towards the door. Mrs. Carter grabbed his arm and pointed at Harpreet walking away and said, "See?"

Harpreet enjoyed the little game she was playing with Abbey. She really wasn't sure how she felt about him, she felt something. She just didn't know what. She wasn't used to a man who ignored her. She was beautiful, intelligent, fun to be with and men were naturally attracted to her. She knew this. She'd been attracting males since junior high school. She didn't understand why he seemed disinterested. Apparently, he wasn't involved with anyone. He wasn't gay…was he? No, he couldn't be. Not the way he watched her walk and the way he admired her legs when she was running. She couldn't figure him out. This is what made him so intriguing. That, plus he was deadly handsome.

She knew he graduated from Virginia Tech and she had a friend who taught in the undergraduate program there. She'd call him to see if he knew anything, or could find someone who knew something of Abbey when he lived there. Her friend, Scott, had tried in vain to date her during their undergraduate years together. But, Harpreet was never interested in Scott as a boyfriend. To her, he was just a good friend.

Scott taught in the math department at Tech and had never heard of Abbey. However, he told Harpreet he'd check around the computer department and get back with her. Scott called her back a couple of days later with some news. Abbey, it seems, was a star in the computer lab and everyone there knew him and had stories to tell. Most told of his genius with computers, programming and formatting. Some told tales of his "blonde addiction."

"Blonde addiction," this was the part that interested Harpreet. She definitely was not blonde. Scott hinted that he might be passing through Winston-Salem next week. Harpreet lied and told him she was going to Atlanta with her friend Dianna, but to make sure he called her the next time he was coming through. She thanked him and hurriedly got off the phone. She had to think.

Chapter 32

JULIETTE WAS GETTING VERY FRUSTRATED WITH HER MOTHER. She knew she was using her father's death as an excuse to keep her around, but that wasn't what was bothering her. She never realized the extent of her mother's drinking, nor the unabashed joy she exhibited in not having her husband around. Her mother would start each morning with either a Bloody Mary or Mimosa, (usually several of both.) She rationalized that tomato juice and orange juice were healthy and therefore good for her.

Then it was two or three glasses of wine for lunch, cocktails in the afternoons, more wine at dinner and full blown liquor shots in the evenings. Her main source of entertainment seemed to be visiting Napa Valley with her friends for wine tasting tours. This was the reason Juliette kept staying around, not because of her grieving mother, but because of her alcoholic mother. She didn't know what to do.

She had no life of her own, outside of activities with her mother as designated driver. They shopped together, had their hair and nails done together, and had lunches with her mother's friends (with wine). They were experiencing all the bliss possible, that an alcoholic mother and heart-broken daughter could have with each other, while still keeping their sanity.

The only thing positive to happen for Juliette was that somehow her art gallery was doing very well. This was good news, but even that made her sad thinking that Martha, of all people, could do a better job at running her gallery than she ever did. She thought Martha would desperately need her financial support to keep the shop going. She was wrong, it was doing very well.

Martha didn't need her. Her mother was using her. She missed her life. She missed Abbey. She was miserable!

The Winston-Salem Journal wanted to do a special on Abbey for their Sunday business section. This concerned Jack Braswell, Lonewolf's president. The more notoriety and publicity Abbey received, the better the chances some larger company would try to steal his money-maker away from him. The Winston-Salem Magazine had also called and wanted an interview with Abbey and Jack Braswell. Normally, the president would love to see his name, and his company's name, in print. But this had him very concerned.

Lonewolf's revenues for the first quarter after hiring Abbey had risen by nearly 70%. Jack Braswell's salary was tied to his company's performance so he had a very vested interest in keeping Abbey at Lonewolf. And, keeping him happy. Very happy.

He asked Abbey to come to his office under the pretense of discussing some new business. When he arrived Jack bounded from behind his teakwood desk and met him at the door in front of the life- sized bronze statue of a wolf, which was the company's mascot. He shook his hand and asked how he was. Abbey said, "I feel fine." Then Jack started with the praise, thanks and superlatives. Abbey finally stopped him and said, "Okay Jack…what's up?" He figured he wanted him to do something for him and was setting him up.

"Nothing, everything's great! I just wanted to show my appreciation for all you've done and personally tell you how much you mean to the company and to me as a friend." He was still not convinced Jack wasn't up to something, until Jack said, "I've got a couple of presents for you that are long overdue. Just to show my appreciation and how much we value you here. First, I want to give you this five year membership to Pine Brook Country Club. It's a great place and I'm sure you'll enjoy playing out there.

Second, I want you to know I've already called payroll and increased your salary to $407,125." Abbey was silent for a few moments, then shook Jack's hand and thanked him. He was aware that the amount of the raise was equal to his original salary demands when he was first negotiating. He was also aware that it was a very generous raise of $92,975. But, he also knew he had earned it.

Jack started telling him about Pine Brook and Abbey cut in and said, "I don't really play golf Jack, I've never had the time or inclination." Jack knew this but had hoped to introduce him to the game and have him join his weekend golf group. He'd gladly kick someone out of the group if he could ingratiate Abbey into his personal fold even further.

Jack insisted they go out to Pine Brook for lunch, so he could show him around. He'd already called ahead and they had the welcoming committee ready and waiting for them. Jack was on the Board of Directors and could arrange virtually anything he wanted at the club. The clubhouse was very nice. The dining room was elegant, yet comfortable and Abbey liked everything he saw. Jack saved his "piece de resistance" for last.

After lunch, he led Abbey to the office of the club president, who was waiting on them, along with the Membership Director, Robyn Warren. Robyn was Jack's ace-in-the-hole. She was not only gorgeous, very personable and intelligent; but she was also single and very, very blonde. Jack had done his homework.

Robyn had the reputation around the club of being the "closer." Anytime men came in to personally inspect the club with thoughts of joining and were introduced to Robyn....game over. Her beauty and charm always closed the deal. No matter how much they raised the initiation fees, once guys met Robyn, they couldn't wait to write her a check, while secretly hoping for a return on their investment at a later date. That, of course, never happened.

Jack excused himself from the grand tour and Robyn led Abbey around the facility and pro shop. Then she got a golf cart and drove him around the course, showing off each of the 18 holes, plus a whole lot of leg. The course itself meant nothing to him. The grass was green and there were geese on the lakes. He was much more impressed with how Robyn maneuvered the golf cart while somehow keeping her skirt from sliding too far up her thigh as she moved her foot from one pedal to the other.

Even though he knew exactly what was happening here, he still enjoyed it. Robyn was delightful, beautiful and very sexy. How could he not like it? When they finished the tour, she gave him her business card and told him to call her anytime if he had any questions or if there was anything she could do to help. Which seemed to him to be a very loaded comment. He thanked her, smiled at her and told her he enjoyed the tour. After he smiled at her, she didn't hear anything else. She too fell under the spell of Abbey.

Chapter 33

EVERYTHING SEEMED TO BE FALLING INTO PLACE for him. His job was very secure, he was a star and making an excellent salary. He'd made several friends around town, including the irrepressible Opie. He'd found Mrs. Carter and Annie Norwood, each of whom gave him the best excuse in the world to continue his passion (or was it a vice) of playing poker. He had it all....except Juliette. Why couldn't he let her go? What was it about her that dwelt in his soul and would not fade away? No matter how many times he said to himself, "She's getting married you idiot! Let it go!" He couldn't.

He was looking forward to the weekend. His plan was to have coffee and a pastry outside of Camino's again on Saturday morning. Consciously hoping that Harpreet would NOT be jogging down the street again, yet subconsciously hoping she would. Before he started his day he read an email from his grandfather, he hadn't heard from him in a couple of days. The message read,

"ONE DAY YOUR LIFE WILL FLASH BEFORE YOUR EYES. MAKE SURE IT'S WORTH WATCHING."

Saturday morning at Camino's, he got his coffee (with cream), and a sweet apple tart and sat outside watching the traffic go by. A young girl was walking a dog with a scarf around its neck. A muscle-bound man and woman were walking towards Gold's Gym. Four young co-eds from either Salem or Wake Forest were strolling carelessly down the sidewalk, none of them talking to each other, all of them texting someone else. Three scruffy looking young dudes were standing at the corner, trying to look bad, but their new Nike sneakers and polished fingernails gave them away (probably Wake students as well). And a variety of other ages, races and sexes (some known, some unknown), were all walking aimlessly up and down 4th street. A day in the life. Some would stop at Camino's, where he was and others just walked on by. All of them trying to see who else was out, or more importantly, who was watching them.

After his second cup of coffee, reading the paper and completing the crossword puzzle, he gave up on seeing Harpreet this morning. He started gathering his stuff and then he saw her jogging down the next block. It was hard to not see those legs. As soon as he saw her, she waved to him. "Dang!" He thought," I wish she hadn't seen me looking at her."

Again, as he watched her running up to his table, he tried in vain not to stare at her legs so that she could tell he was staring. It was a vain attempt. She came up to his table and asked, "How do you like my new running shorts? I noticed you were staring at them."

"I wasn't staring at your running shorts Harpreet."

"Oh, so you were staring at my legs again, huh?"

"No, I wasn't; I was simply…."

174

But she interrupted, "It's okay if you were staring, I take that as a compliment. I see you've already had your pastry this morning. Was it good?"

He was trying his best to come back with something snappy, but could only respond with, "Yes, it was." Why couldn't he think of something?

She said, "Well, just be careful with the calories, you're a little too young for middle-aged spread."

He had her now, he quickly told her, "I get plenty of exercise during the week. I play tennis at Hanes Park."

"Oh, that's great." She said, "We should play sometime, I love tennis, it would be fun."

"Well, I don't really play games with people, I just hit balls."

She looked at him for few seconds and replied, "So you don't want to play me in tennis? Is that right?"

"Right," he said, "I don't play matches."

She looked intently at him and said, "I don't blame you. If I couldn't beat a girl, I wouldn't play either." And without waiting for a reply, she was off and running down the street.

Not even the sight of her "bottom," as Mrs. Carter described it, could calm the angst he felt at having once again been bettered in this all too familiar patter with Harpreet. He thought to himself once more, "There is no way on God's green earth that woman is Indian!"

When he got back to his condo there was a message from Robyn Warren asking him to call her back at his convenience. That was interesting. Lonewolf had already paid his membership for five years, so there was nothing left to sell him on. He tried to forget about Harpreet as he dialed up the country club. It wasn't easy.

Robyn Warren told him the club was having a "New Members" get together Sunday night, and she invited Abbey to attend. Drinks and appetizers would be available and the chance to familiarize yourself with the club and with both recent members as well as long time members, who would be around to answer questions. He initially thought she was just calling him and was a little disappointed when she told him she had a "lot of other calls to make." But that was okay, he told her he'd love to attend and would see her Sunday night.

As soon as the call was over, his mind instantly switched back to Harpreet. His thoughts drifted from her legs, to her "bottom," and to why and how she seemed to always get the best of him. He also thought of why he was always thinking about her. He was unsure if he was attracted to her as a friend, or romantically, or as a verbal opponent he wanted to best in a discussion. Or, all three. Or, none. She was confusing him and he wasn't used to that.

To work out his anxiety, he gathered his racket and went to Hanes Park to hit some tennis balls. He could beat her if he wanted to, any time at all. He just chose not to. That was his choice and there was nothing wrong with it. He could beat her. He hit balls until he noticed his shirt was wet. Had he been sweating? She got the best of him in conversations and now she was making him sweat?

He chose to stay in that night and think. A nice fire and sitting out on his balcony always calmed him down and helped clarify his thoughts. Not this night. Even after two glasses of Riesling, he still couldn't control his thoughts. No matter how hard he tried, he could not—he simply could not—stop thinking about Juliette. He consciously tried to imagine scenarios with Harpreet, and even Robyn, but he kept coming back to Juliette. All he could think of was, "What am I going to do?"

He woke early Sunday morning, in fact, he didn't sleep well all night. It was a relief to finally get up. He drank coffee, he toasted a bagel, he read each section of the Sunday paper and he still had two and half hours before church. He went down to the little gym there at his condo and walked on the treadmill while listening to his ipod. Hopefully, the wistful voices of Colbie Caillat, Tristan Prettyman and Nikki Bluhm could take his mind off women. These probably weren't the best choices one could make under the circumstances.

He had decided there was no way he would let Harpreet get the best of him today. He would be ready and would not be trapped by any of her verbal games. He felt good. He felt confidant. He felt like his old self. "I'm back!" He thought. He arrived for church a bit early and Mrs. Carter wasn't there yet so he waited for her in the vestibule. After a few minutes she came in and was happy to see that a handsome young man was there to greet her.

As he was in the process of telling her how nice she looked today, Harpreet came up the steps as well. Mrs. Carter said, "Oh, look. Here's your friend. Harpreet, you look beautiful today. Doesn't she Abbey?" But before he could answer (and he didn't know exactly how to answer that), Mrs. Carter continued, "Harpreet, please come and sit with us, I'm sure Abbey would love it." Again, before he could utter a single word, Harpreet answered, "Thank you Mrs. Carter, I appreciate the thought, but I don't think I'm nearly blonde enough for your friend here."

And with that, she turned and walked up the stairs to the balcony. Abbey, who had yet to open his mouth, and Mrs. Carter both watched her climb the steps. When she passed from view, Mrs. Carter looked up at him and said, "If I could walk like that, I'd have Brad Pitt as my date tonight." Abbey, who had still not spoken, did not know what to say. He couldn't believe it had happened to him again.

As Mrs. Carter slept on his shoulder during the sermon, he practiced good comebacks he would dazzle Harpreet with after church. He had little idea what the preacher's message was, but had a great idea what his verbal response would be after church. He was primed and ready as he walked Mrs. Carter out of the sanctuary. He waited in the vestibule, he lingered on the steps, he loafed in front of the church. But no Harpreet. By her absence, she had beaten him again.

He was both confused and perplexed regarding his feelings. Think for yourself, he kept repeating. He opened his computer to write a message to his grandfather, he knew his response and words would somehow ground him and make sense out of things. He wrote, "Grandfather, I'm having a difficult time understanding life in today's world. I wish things were as simple now as they were when you grew up. Have I changed that much, or has the world changed?"

It took a little less than an hour, and the reply came back short and succinct,

BACK IN THE 60'S, DURING MY YOUTH, PEOPLE TOOK ACID TO MAKE THE WORLD WEIRD. NOW THE WORLD IS WEIRD AND PEOPLE TAKE PROZAC TO MAKE IT NORMAL.

JUST KEEP BEING YOURSELF, AS A WISE MAN ONCE SAID, 'ALL THINGS MUST PASS.'

Chapter 34

HE WAS LOOKING FORWARD to the social gathering Sunday night at Pine Brook Country Club. He'd get to meet more new members, be able to talk with Robyn Warren again and most importantly, get his mind off Harpreet and Juliette.

There were twenty-two people at the party, all with wives or girlfriends except for him and Robyn. He smiled a lot and spelled his name to nearly everyone there. Why couldn't his parents have named him Bob? He heard stories of birdies and bogies and of snakes and wild tantrums and fights on the golf course. He was asked twenty-one times what his handicap was and nineteen times what equipment he used. He tried to be polite. It wasn't easy.

He noticed how Robyn floated from one group to another, laughing and smiling and making everyone feel at ease. She was the consummate hostess as well as being the most attractive woman in the room——by far. He collected business cards from nearly all the men in attendance and was told to call them if he ever needed any help from: a lawyer, two bankers, a home builder, an accountant and two retired guys (one guy actually gave him a business card that read "Retired.")

He also met a salesman for Hanesbrands underwear, who said he knew Michael Jordon. And, he met a vice president from

Krispy Kreme (who gave him several coupons for free doughnuts). There was a dentist there who wore a UNC Tarheel blue blazer with matching baby blue tie. And finally, he met a plumber (yes, a plumber) who told the best joke of the night about a talking parrot. Each and every one of them gathering for the love of golf. All of them wondering why this guy with the funny name, who didn't play golf, nor own any golf clubs, was in attendance. Abbey was wondering the same thing himself.

He found out why he was in attendance near the end of the party. As the lawyers and doctors and salesmen and plumber all started saying their goodbyes and drifting homeward, Robyn asked him if he would help her with something in the next room. As soon as he walked in the room, she turned around and laid a lip-lock on him, the likes of which he'd seldom experienced.

He couldn't speak because her tongue was halfway down his throat. Not that he minded. It just took him by surprise. After disengaging herself, she looked up at him, winked and walked back into the party. He lingered a bit at the reception before heading towards the exit with the Krispy Kreme guy, when Robyn called to him and said she needed a word.

He walked back in towards her and she came close to him and said, in a sultry, sexy voice, "I hope you enjoyed that. I was wondering what you're doing the rest of the night?" Abbey said, "Well, I didn't have any other plans, I was just going home. Did you want to go somewhere and have a drink or something?"

She grinned and replied, "Well, since it's now just the two of us, I was hoping you'd invite me back to your place." He wasn't expecting this. He was used to this type of reaction from other women, he just didn't think it would happen this evening with Robyn. "That would be very nice, I have a bottle or two of wine we could sample." She said, "Let me finish up here quickly and I'll follow you in my car."

When they arrived at his place, he lit a fire and brought a bottle of Pinot Grigio out to the balcony. It wasn't his favorite wine, but he'd found that most women enjoyed it. He poured them each a glass and Robyn started talking. And continued talking and talking and talking. She told him about her job, about her family, about her college years, about her past boyfriends, about her favorite restaurants, about her wardrobe. After nearly an hour of non-stop, one-sided conversation, she asked him where his restroom was. He pointed it out to her, grateful for a break in the maelstrom of jibberish. He was feverishly wondering how he could gracefully end this evening when he heard her calling him from inside the condo.

He looked inside and she was standing there wearing nothing but a very provocative grin. She said, "I want you," as she motioned for him to follow her into his bedroom. "Well," he thought, "no wonder Pine Brook is such a popular country club."

Robyn didn't stay the entire night, thankfully. He could only assume that she had nothing else to tell him about. After her initial lustful desires were satisfied, she started telling him of her days as a cheerleader. Then, she told him of her first pet and her favorite cat; then, about her sister (who was married to a dud of a husband). On and on she went. She told him of her first sexual encounter, her first round of golf, her first trip to New York, her favorite birthday present. Sometime, early in the morning, during the description of her workout routines, he dozed off.

He wasn't sure how long he napped, but when he awoke she was describing how her apartment was decorated. Then she said, "Oh Abbey, I just love talking to you, we have the absolute best conversations don't we?" "Umm, yes. We sure do Robyn." She jumped out of bed, got dressed, kissed him and told him she'd call him tomorrow. Then she giggled and said, "Wait, I guess I mean later today." And she was off.

He got up to make sure the door was locked. Securely. He turned on his computer, thankful for something that couldn't talk back to him. He had another message from his grandfather,

"THE PURSUIT OF HAPPINESS IS THE CHIEF CAUSE OF UNHAPPINESS."

He was unhappy. Why did she talk so much? Why is she so boring? Why couldn't she be more of this? And less of that? Why does she act like she does? Tell me why oh why couldn't she…..be like Juliette?????

He'd never really complained about things and the state of his life to his grandfather before. He'd never had reason to. All his life, so far, things had gone just as he hoped they would. His conversations with his grandfather were almost exclusively informational on his part. He would tell of his job, or school, or his parents and then he'd always wait to hear what advice and words of wisdom his grandfather would impart.

But now, he felt lost. He needed to tell someone of his troubles, his heartache, his great disappointment in losing

Juliette. He needed to bare his soul. He could never talk with his parents about these things. He didn't really have any close friends in Winston-Salem. He couldn't talk to Harpreet—heck, she was part of the problem. His boss was his boss. Opie was his friend, but not that kind of friend, yet. No, his grandfather was the only one he could confide in. So he started writing.

He didn't leave anything out. He was as honest with his feelings as he knew how to be. The problem was that some issues still confused him. He truly wasn't sure how he felt about Harpreet, he couldn't even describe it accurately to his grandfather. She was an enigma, a puzzle, an algorithm he was totally incapable of solving at this point in time. Juliette was not. He was heartbreakingly honest about her with his grandfather.

He closed by apologizing for this unusual email. He hated to bother his grandfather with his personal issues and even suggested he should've found someone else to share his troubles and burdens with. He went to work, periodically checking his emails. Nothing. He now wished he'd not written anything. He was a little embarrassed by his admissions and hoped his grandfather wouldn't be too disappointed in him.

After work, he came straight home. He didn't hit tennis balls. He didn't walk on the treadmill. He didn't even want a "Blarney Burger" from Finnegan's Wake. Instead, he poured himself a glass of Chambourcin as punishment. He didn't like Chambourcin, but he'd drink it as he stared at the blank computer screen and waited.

And he did wait. This was unusual. His grandfather seldom left his house, except to go to the church he pastored. He was always at home and has certainly had time to read the email. This was not good, not good at all. "Why did I send that email?" He started abusing himself for being so thoughtless. As he finally finished the glass of wine, and it wasn't easy, his computer dinged with an email. He closed one eye and squinted with the other one to see who it was from. Oh boy, it's from him. Suddenly, apprehension overflowed within him, He thought about not even reading it, but he had to. He had no choice.

"ABHINANDAN, I'M GLAD YOU CONFIDED IN ME. YOU CAN ALWAYS TRUST ME OVER OTHERS. 90% OF OTHER PEOPLE DON'T CARE THAT YOU HAVE PROBLEMS; THE OTHER 10% ARE GLAD YOU HAVE THEM! LOVE IS DIFFICULT AND THERE ARE NO EASY SOLUTIONS. THERE IS NOTHING I CAN TELL YOU TO MAKE THIS ANY BETTER (THOUGH I WOULD LOVE TO MEET JULIETTE AND HARPREET BOTH).

I AM GOING TO GIVE YOU MY 3 RULES FOR LIVING HOWEVER. APPLY THEM IN ALL SITUATIONS AND ALL CIRCUMSTANCES AND YOU WILL BE SUCCESSFUL IN WHATEVER POSITION YOU MAY FIND YOURSELF IN.

1. DO WHAT'S RIGHT. ALWAYS DO THE RIGHT THING. IT'S NEVER THE WRONG TIME TO DO THE RIGHT THING; AND IT'S NEVER THE RIGHT TIME TO DO THE WRONG THING.
2. DO EVERYTHING TO THE BEST OF YOUR ABILITY: JOB, MARRIAGE, GOLF, FISHING...EVERYTHING!
3. SHOW PEOPLE YOU CARE.

IF YOU AREN'T FOLLOWING THESE PRINCIPLES, THEN YOU NEED TO CHANGE YOUR LIFE. ABHINANDAN, MY SON, WHEN 'YOU' CHANGE, EVERYTHING ELSE CHANGES."

Chapter 35

IT WAS A LONG WEEK AT WORK. Robyn Warren sent him an email every day hinting that she'd like to get together again. He ignored the first three, then lied to her saying he had to go out of town. Since he wanted to somewhat follow his grandfather's advice, and "do the right thing," he decided he would get out of town and drive back up to Cherokee. He didn't really need to win anything just yet. He was still in good shape with the Mrs. Carter and Annie Norwood fund, but he was a little concerned Robyn might show up free as a bird, at his doorstep.

He arrived at Harrah's Cherokee Casino and went straight to the poker tables. He stayed away from the high stakes room, he just wanted to pass the time and get his mind off things. The problem was that he couldn't get his mind off things. He was so pre-occupied with thoughts of Juliette and Harpreet he could never get accurate reads on the other players.

He started losing. Then he started pressing and losing more. Sometimes the cards are just not good. This night, the cards were not kind to him and he could not concentrate enough to formulate "tells" on the other players. If he had a pair of queens, then some farmer from Trap Hill had a pair of kings. When he had a set of three, a guy with a Mohawk and ring in his nose had a straight.

That's the way the night went for him. He even ordered his usual "Iron Maiden" and the waitress brought him a "Cape Cod" by mistake. It was that kind of night. A little after 1:00 AM he called it an evening. He had lost $3,137 while never betting anything larger than $50 all night. He cancelled his room reservation and decided he'd make the four hour drive back to Winston instead. Maybe church in the morning would help soothe his frustrations. Maybe he could not think of a girl, maybe he could think for no one.

He caught a couple hours of sleep before church and arrived to find Mrs. Carter already there, sitting with Harpreet. Wasn't this just dandy? He slid in next to Mrs. Carter with Harpreet on the other side of her. Before he could say anything to Mrs. Carter, or ask how she was, she leaned over to him and whispered, "Did you notice the short skirt she has on?" Well...he had, but he wasn't going to admit it to Mrs. Carter. "No ma'am, I only noticed how beautiful you look today."

"Well then Abhinandan, you're blind!" He just shook his head as Harpreet then leaned over to say, "I hope you don't mind if I sit with you today, Mrs. Carter insisted." "Certainly not," he responded, "you can sit with us anytime if it makes you happy." When she heard, "...if it makes you happy." she got up and left.

Mrs. Carter looked up at him trying to say something, but words abandoned her. He looked back at her and said, "What?" She finally said, "I'll never understand men." Fortunately for him, the choir started singing 'How Great Thou Art.' He didn't dare turn around to look for Harpreet. Initially, he didn't think Mrs. Carter was going to take her usual nap, maybe she was too incensed with him. But, nature took over and she dozed during the last portion of the message.

He was relieved not to find Harpreet waiting for him as he walked Mrs. Carter out. Maybe this wasn't going to be as bad as he thought it would. He was looking forward to going back home and taking a short nap of his own. As he was unlocking his car door in the church parking lot, he heard the click, click, click of a woman in high heels walking very fast. It was not a sound he was wishing for.

He turned around and before she was within ten feet of him she started, "It most certainly DID NOT make me happy to be sitting with you today! I did it as a personal favor to Mrs. Carter. But trust me," and she said his name verrry slowly, "AB HI NAN DAN, it will never happen again! In fact, I'll also find a new place to run on Saturday mornings and you can find someone else's legs to drool over. Goodbye!!"

He didn't realize it was possible for a woman to walk that fast in high heels. But unanticipatedly, he also realized something else very important, he did indeed like the way she walked. He liked it a lot.

After church, Harpreet went back to her home fuming. She totally forgot that her friend Dianna was coming over. Unfortunately for Dianna, she walked into a maelstrom of fury and wrath from her normally calm and collected friend. She said, "Okay, start at the beginning and tell me what happened."

She listened, and she listened, and she listened some more. Then Dianna said, "Is that it?"

"No!" Harpreet shouted, "I haven't told you the worst of it. After he sat down in church he looked at me said I could sit with them—and get this Dianna— 'if it made me happy.' Like I only sat there to make ME happy, like it was a privilege for me to be able to sit with the Crown Prince of snobbery! If Mrs. Carter hadn't been there I would have slapped him back till Tuesday."

"Well, what did you do then?"

"I was so upset that I just couldn't stay in church, so I went out and sat in my car."

Dianna looked quizzically at her and said, "You really showed him, didn't you Harpy?"

"No! I mean...that's not what I meant. I waited till after church when he came out to his car then I told him what I thought of him and warned him to never come near me again."

Dianna was silent a few moments, then said, "And you did all this because he said, 'if it makes you happy?'

Harpreet looked at her and thought for a few seconds and finally said, "Yes. What do you think about all of it?"

Dianna nodded, arched her eyebrows and answered, "Yep, you've definitely got yourself a boyfriend!"

When he got home from church, he was still perplexed and somewhat shaken from the verbal assault Harpreet had leveled on him in the parking lot. But, he was tired, so he stretched out on the couch, closed his eyes and thought of more pleasant things. Like the sight of her walking away in the church parking lot.

He'd been asleep about forty-five minutes when the phone woke him. He was still a little drowsy and wasn't exactly sure who was speaking. He asked, "Is this Mrs. Carter?" "Yes Abhinandan, of course it is. How many other 90 year old women do you have calling you?"

"I'm just surprised Mrs. Carter, how did you get my number?" "You filled out a guest registration card your first Sunday with us and put your address and phone number on it so the pastor could contact you. The head deacon in the church has been our friend for over fifty years, he got it for me. I hope you don't mind me calling. You don't have a woman there with you ...do you?"

"No ma'am, I don't. And, it's nice to hear from you. Is there something I can do for you?" "Yes," she said, "I want you to come to dinner at my house tonight. I'll be very disappointed if you can't come, but I'll understand if you have a hot date tonight."

"No, ma'am, I don't have a hot date. I'd love to come over, thank you very much." She giggled and said, "I didn't think you did. Be here about 7:00, I can't stay up too late, you know how us old people are."

"I'll be there, thanks again. Can I bring anything?" She paused and answered, "Just your smile, make sure you bring that. See you tonight Abhinandan, bye."

Normally, he would've brought a nice bottle of wine when invited to dinner. But, tonight, he settled for a fresh bouquet of flowers instead. Mrs. Carter lived in an old house on S. Main Street, not far from Old Salem and Salem College. There was an old garage, or workshop out back, that looked as though it was falling into disrepair. He figured it was probably where Mr. Carter piddled around before he became sick.

He opened the screen and knocked on a solid wood door. It opened and Abbey stood looking at a rather plump, plain looking girl, about 25 years old. She said, "My name's Gloria, I'm the granddaughter. Come in please, Nana is in the kitchen." Gloria had her mousy brown hair pulled back into a tight bun and waddled a little like a duck when she walked. She led him into the parlor and sat across from him staring at him. She didn't say anything, she just stared at him.

Abbey finally said, "So, do you live near hear Gloria?" "No." she answered. More silence. "Well, where do you live, if you don't mind me asking?" "Kernersville." Then, more silence.

"Are you still in school Gloria?" "No."

"So what kind of work do you do then?" But she didn't answer this question, she just kept staring at him.

He finally said, "Are you okay Gloria?" She squirmed a little. She pulled her dress down even further than the mid-calf level it already was. She pushed her glasses back up from where they'd slipped down her nose. Then her face turned red and she said, "You're more handsome than Nana said you were." With that, she quickly got up and waddled towards the kitchen.

Mrs. Carter soon came in and dinner was served. She had prepared fried chicken, pinto beans, white rice and homemade cornbread, with peach cobbler for dessert. It was all wonderful. Mrs. Carter told stories and tales of her youth and of travels with her husband. Abbey loved hearing them all. Gloria never opened her mouth except to clean her plate and ask for seconds.

After coffee was served and the table cleared, Gloria told her Nana that she had to be going. She asked her if she'd be okay. Mrs. Carter looked at Abbey and asked, "Are you going to behave yourself young man?" He smiled, Mrs. Carter laughed and Gloria blushed. After she left, Abbey said, "You have a lovely granddaughter Mrs. Carter."

"She's overweight, plain, mousy and as dumb as Herbert Hoover. But I love her." Mrs. Carter didn't expect him to argue with her and he didn't. Then she looked at him and said, "Is this the sort of girl you're looking for Abhinandan?"

He really didn't want to hurt Mrs. Carter's feelings, so he said nothing. She continued, "I know you're not interested in Gloria. Who would be? My question is why you're not interested in Harpreet?"

Now he really didn't know what to say. She kept looking at him, she cocked her head from one side to the other, finally saying, "Well?"

"Mrs. Carter, I don't know what to say. I don't know how to explain it."

She said, "Well, I know you like her, I've seen the way you look at her legs and how she walks. And, Lord knows, she's beautiful. What's not to like?"

"It's complicated." This was all he could offer. She took a few seconds to absorb this nonsense, then said, "There's another woman isn't there?" By his silence, she knew she was right. She finally said, "Okay, tell me about her. What's her name? Where does she live? What does she do? I bet she's blonde isn't she? That's what Harpreet meant in church that day about not being blonde enough for you. Now I get it!"

"No ma'am, you don't understand. There used to be another woman, and she was blonde. But she moved away and is marrying someone else. The problem is that I don't think I'm over her yet. In fact, I know I'm not. Harpreet is indeed very attractive, but I can't seem to let go of Juliette. That's her name."

They talked of Juliette and of Harpreet and of loves lost and loves won the rest of the evening. Eventually, Mrs. Carter laid her hand on his arm and said, "Son, there are only four questions of value in life: What is sacred? Of what is the spirit made? What is worth living for? And, what is worth dying for? The answer to each of these is the same….only love." They sat in silence for a few moments longer until he could sense Mrs. Carter was getting a little tired, so he excused himself. She hugged him on the front porch and told him to never give up hope. He wished he could believe her.

Chapter 36

THE FOLLOWING SATURDAY MORNING, Abbey went to Camino's, got his pastry and coffee and sat outside watching traffic lazily pass by. However, the only thing he seemed to notice was the absence of a really nice set of legs in running shorts. He'd even practiced an apology he would use to smooth things over with Harpreet. Oh well, it was for the best, he thought. He drank more coffee than he usually did, wasting time, enjoying his own company, letting his mind wander in unknown directions. The problem was it kept coming back to the one direction he had no control over.

Finally, he decided to go back home. He would check on his acquaintances through cyber space, just to make sure everyone was okay. His grandfather had sent an email since he'd been gone. He hoped it would somehow touch his loneliness and comfort him with words of wisdom. It read,

"SOME PEOPLE WALK IN THE RAIN, OTHERS JUST GET WET."

He read this message 10 times, 20 times...he still didn't understand it. Sometimes his grandfather was apparently so cosmic that normal human beings weren't privileged enough to share his enlightenment.

He hacked into Mrs. Carter's bank account to make sure she was okay. She was. He checked on Annie Norwood and she wasn't okay. He needed to help her again. He deleted several more emails from Robyn Warren. How long was this going to last? Then, he thought he'd check on Juliette's art gallery. He wondered if she'd be selling it now that she was getting married.

Knowing Martha as he did, he was a little surprised it was still open. She didn't seem to be the most astute businesswoman he'd ever met. He assumed the gallery would be closing soon. Martha had told him that when Juliette left she told her to make all the decisions and that any profit it made would be hers. But it had never been very profitable, even when Juliette was running it with help from her parents.

He found that Juliette was still listed as the owner and then to his amazement saw that the gallery had done over $73,000 worth of business in the last two months. Martha was the only employee there now. The only other expenses were the rent, utilities and upkeep. He investigated everything there was to look at. He found Martha's banking records online and saw that she was depositing huge sums of money each week into her account. All of it in cash deposits. People didn't buy expensive pieces of art with cash. He thought, "Martha, what on earth are you doing?"

Not that he cared that much what Martha was doing. But if something fishy was going on at the gallery (and it obviously was), he didn't want Juliette to get dragged into it. She may be marrying someone else, but he still cared for her and didn't want Martha hurting her. He had to find out what was going on, without letting anyone know he was trying to find out what was going on.

He didn't want to actually go in the gallery himself, he still didn't want to be confronted with news of Juliette and her marriage. He needed someone to help him snoop, someone he could trust, someone who knew Winston. He needed someone like Opie. But would Opie help him? Was he even good enough friends to ask for this sort of help? He went to Finnegan's for dinner and tried something different—Bangers & Mash.

It was good, but even the Guinness tasted a little funny tonight. The thought of somehow bringing Opie into his scheme was weighing on his mind. Opie came to his table and told him a joke about a talking dog, which surprisingly was very funny. But Abbey couldn't pull the trigger, he just couldn't ask Opie to get involved. Not even a table full of Wake coeds (most of them blonde) could keep his attention. He left the Guinness half full and the dinner half eaten. He had to think.

As he was walking up Trade Street towards 4th Street, where his condo was, he noticed a sign for a lawyer on one of the store fronts at 401-A Trade Street. It caught his attention because it was the same name as one of his computer engineering professors at Virginia Tech, Curtis Bland. As he chuckled over this coincidence, he also noticed in small print, the name of another tenant in the building at 401-B Trade Street, Desmond Jones, Private Investigator. Yes, a private detective, this was exactly what he needed.

He typed the phone number in his mobile so he wouldn't forget it and instantly felt much better about everything. He anxiously called Mr. Jones' office the next morning, but only got a voice recorder. He kept calling him all day, but got the recorder each time. He didn't want to leave a message, but he wanted action, he wanted to get moving on this.

After work, he walked down to Mr. Jones' office. He had no plan, but was impatient and needed to do something. He went in the building and took the stairs up to the second floor and saw a door straight ahead marked "Desmond Jones, Private Investigations." He knew the office was empty because he'd just called it from the street, but he knocked on the door anyway. As soon as he knocked, he heard movement inside and could see through the smoked glass that someone was approaching the door.

The door opened and a short, balding man with a thin mustache said, "Can I help you?" Abbey looked at him and said, "Are you Desmond Jones?" The guy looked up at him and answered, "No, I'm James Bond, Moneypenny's out to lunch. Of course I'm Desmond Jones, who else would be in my office?"

Abbey said, "Well, I've been calling your office and no one ever answered. I thought you might be out of town."

"Do I look like I'm out of town? What do you want?"

Abbey had had just about enough of his surliness and thought there would probably be other, less abrasive private detectives in town, so he answered, "No, you don't look like you're out of town. You look like an out-of-work elf waiting on Santa to bring you some Jack Daniels." They both stared at each other for about fifteen seconds and Mr. Jones finally said, "Well what were you expecting, Sean, freaking Connery? Come in and shut the door."

He did come in and sat in a plush chair, across a huge desk from Mr. Jones, in a well decorated office with several original paintings hanging on the walls. Mr. Jones said, "Well?"

Abbey replied, " I wasn't expecting such rude behavior from someone in your type of business."

"Well, we're even then. I wasn't expecting a well-dressed, rich Indian who has woman problems to be knocking on my door."

"How do you know I'm Indian? And what makes you think I have woman problems?"

Desmond Jones just snickered at him and said, "Because, Mahatma, I'm a detective and I'm not stupid!"

Abbey couldn't decide whether to get up and leave or start laughing. Then Desmond said, "Just tell me what your problem is and I'll let you know if I want to help you. But I have to be honest with you Ghandi, I really jack my prices up to rich foreigners."

Without a pause, Abbey answered, "I'll tell you what I need help with, then I'll decide IF I will let you help me. And if I do let you help me, I'll only pay you what you're worth. And from what I've seen so far, you'll be working very cheap."

Desmond Jones looked across the desk at him. Abbey returned the look. Then Desmond stood up and extended his hand and Abbey shook it. They never discussed a fee. Abbey then gave him a short history of Juliette and the art gallery and what he knew of Martha. He didn't tell him anything about his personal history with Juliette. He told him he wanted to find out what was going on at the gallery and how Martha was making so much money.

After he finished, Desmond stood up and said, "Give me your contact information and I'll be back in touch with you in a few days. And one other thing Nehru, don't tell anyone you know me, or that you've seen me."

Abbey said, "Okay." And as he opened the door to leave, he looked back at Desmond Jones and said, "Please give Molly my regards." He smiled all the way down the steps.

The advantage of being short, balding and nondescript, as Desmond Jones was, was that hardly anyone notices you. It's easy to blend in. It's easy to become anonymous and almost invisible. This helped make Desmond very good at his job. Cheating husbands and wives seldom noticed him. Employees who were stealing never paid any attention to the mousy-looking guy over there in the corner. And certainly, Martha paid no attention to the little guy in plaid Bermuda shorts and flip flops casually walking around the gallery.

She wasn't going to be wasting her time on someone like him, who obviously was not going to be purchasing any works of art. You were right Martha. He wasn't there to purchase any works of art. He was there to observe. Desmond may not have looked like he knew anything, but he was very intelligent. People always took him for granted, and this is what always what got people in trouble with him. And like he told Abbey, he was good at his job.

He had a small hidden camera with him and unnoticed by anyone else, he took pictures of nearly every painting hanging on the walls. He knew a little about art, he'd had to testify in divorce cases about paintings and he'd paid attention to the experts when they testified. He had a few original paintings of his own, nearly all from local Winston-Salem artists.

He thought it was odd that every single painting hanging in the gallery was an original. Not one reproduction or lithograph— all originals. He didn't recognize any of the artists but he made sure he photographed their names as well. When he got back to his office he googled the artist's names, Becca Bernstein, Evan Gruzis, Kadar Brock and Greg Simkins. Although he had never heard of them, they were each nationally known artists.

He thought this was all a little odd. Why would these nationally known artists all have their originals hanging in a little shop in Winston-Salem, instead of New York or Los Angeles? He then googled each individual painting and not to his surprise, found that the originals had indeed been hanging in New York or Los Angeles galleries before each had been sold to private collectors. The question now was: does Martha actually know that the paintings she's selling are fakes? Desmond almost assuredly knew the answer was "yes."

Chapter 37

JULIETTE HAD HER MIND MADE UP, she was going back home to Winston-Salem. She knew her mother was using her simply because she didn't want to be alone. She was tired of all the parties and veiled attempts by her mother to set her up with young men from California. She was sick to death of being her mother's designated driver after her wine lunches and afternoon cocktail parties.

She also decided she would confront Ian when she came home and end his blackmailing dominance of her once-and-for-all. She wanted to be away from her mother, away from Ian and back home, where her heart was.

She told her mother she was leaving early one morning, even before the first mimosa of the day. Her mother pitched a fit. She tried her best to lay guilt trips on Juliette. She tried crying. She tried pleading. Juliette had become immune to all her mother's ploys. Even when her mother threatened to cut off her allowance, Juliette stayed the course. She was going home. She did concede to stay two more weeks because her mother had planned a trip to Hawaii as a family, Juliette and her brother. But as soon as they returned, she was leaving. There was no changing her mind.

Chapter 38

DESMOND JONES WAITED TWO DAYS before he told Abbey what he knew. He wanted him to think he'd spent a lot more time "investigating" the whole affair at the gallery. Abbey came by his office after work and knocked on the door. Desmond yelled at him to come in, he didn't get up. He was eating a hot dog from a street vendor, and drinking a Royal Crown Cola, a drink Abbey was unfamiliar with.

Abbey walked in the door and smelled onions—a lot of onions. Desmond, with his mouth half full, said, "Sit down Geronimo. I've got some news for you." Abbey half-grinned and replied, "I'm not that kind of Indian. And what is that you're drinking?"

"I bought it out on the street, sorry, I don't have another one."

"I didn't actually want one, I just wondered if it helped aid with the digestion of two pounds of onions?" Both men tried their best not to smile. Abbey was unsuccessful.

Desmond finally said, "Your little girlfriend at the gallery has got herself a thriving little business going on over there. If you don't mind the illegal stuff."

"What do you mean, 'illegal stuff'? What is she doing?"

"She's selling fake paintings as the real thing. They put people away for long periods of time for stuff like that. If you want to continue your little 'kissy, kissy with miss prissy', then you'd better tell her to stop what she's doing, and hope no one finds out about all the paintings she's already sold."

"She's not my girlfriend. Are you implying that the paintings hanging in the gallery right now are all fake?"

"No, the paintings are real. Someone did a magnificent job with them. What's fake is the name of the artist that's signed on each of them. I checked and each of the original paintings has either been sold to private collectors, or is in some gallery in New York or L.A. Your little girlfriend has a very talented painter friend who is painting these reproductions, then signing fake names of the original artists on them. Then she's selling them as the real thing at a very, very reduced rate."

He silently thought about this while Desmond finished his hot dog. He finally said, "Well, she knows a lot of artists, I guess it is possible she's doing this."

"It ain't POSSIBLE, Sitting Bull! She's DOING it! She might think she's smart, but trust me, someone who bought one of those fakes will try to re-sell it one day. And when that happens, your little princess will lose her gallery, lose all her money and most importantly, lose her freedom for 7-10 years!

Suddenly, Abbey needed a drink of water, badly. He asked Desmond if he had a water fountain, or anything else to drink. Desmond said, "No, here take a sip of this." And pushed his RC Cola can towards him. The bale of cotton that had exploded in Abbey's mouth simply wasn't dry enough to force him to take a "sip" of onion tainted RC Cola. He said, "No thanks, I'll call you tomorrow. Don't do anything until you hear from me."

He got up and laid an envelope on the desk with $2,000 in it. Desmond didn't open it, but was hoping there was at least $1,000 in it. He slid it in his desk drawer, looked at Abbey as he was leaving and said, "Good luck Abhinandan."

He started walking back home, passing the hot dog cart on the way, they really did smell good. In fact, they smelled so good, he turned around, went back and ordered two "all the way, except onions, and a Diet Pepsi." He drank half the Diet Pepsi immediately and ate both hot dogs before he arrived home at the Nissen Building. He had to do something. He just didn't know what. He could not do nothing and let Juliette's gallery possibly get into big trouble because of that crazy, greedy Martha.

He sat out on the balcony, had a glass of wine and stared out at the old knob of Pilot Mountain. Again, it just stared back at him, silent as a graveyard. It would not share its secrets, nor dispense any of the wisdom it had undoubtedly accumulated these past six thousand years. Why must it be so selfish?

His mind wandered and he thought of a few things his grandfather had emailed him over the last few months.

"ALL THAT IS NECESSARY FOR EVIL TO SUCCEED IS THAT GOOD MEN DO NOTHING."

And

"ALWAYS DO THE RIGHT THING."

The next afternoon he went back to see Desmond Jones, who wasn't in his office. So he went back to the street and had another hot dog, this time with a Royal Crown Cola. He sat on a bench outside the "Yellow Submarine Arts and Crafts Shop" and waited. The pedestrian traffic here was a much more eclectic mix than outside Camino's. He saw girls and guys with blue hair, green hair and no hair. There were girls who looked like guys, guys who looked like girls, and couples (men/women, women/women, men/men and some whose gender was totally unknown to him). He enjoyed taking it all in.

He was admiring a shapely young lady walking down the street who was wearing a potato sack made into a dress. She had tattoos completely covering her right arm and leg, whereas her left appendages were completely bare of ink. As he was admiring her, Desmond tapped him on the shoulder and said, "C'mon up Kemosabe, if you can tear yourself away from the local scenery."

Desmond had bought himself a couple of onion slathered hot dogs and an RC Cola. He didn't offer anything to Abbey. He looked over at him, took a big bite of hot dog and mumbled, "Now what?" Abbey began explaining his plan and what he wanted Desmond to do. Desmond just kept eating and sipping his RC. When he finished, Desmond looked at him, burped, and said, "Okay Vijay, I'll do it."

Abbey said, "When? And, I'm not Vijay Armritraj."

Desmond took his final sip of RC and answered, " Maybe, but you want to be. I'll do it tomorrow."

Abbey laid another envelope on his desk and started for the door. He looked back at Desmond and said, "Don't let me down."

The next day Desmond put on a suit and a hairpiece, picked up his empty briefcase and his Lone Ranger Official Fan Club membership card from the 1960's and left his office. Martha was in the gallery drinking a mocha latte when he walked in. She put her cup down and said, as cheerily as she could that early in the morning, "Hello, can I help you with anything?"

"Martha, my dear, you certainly can." Desmond continued, " You can tell me who's painting all these forgeries you have here in your shop?" Martha did not speak—she couldn't speak. She could barely breathe. Desmond laid his briefcase down, reached inside his coat pocket and flashed his very official looking Lone Ranger membership card at her. It had a huge star imprinted on it, that's why Desmond used it, and it was very effective in certain situations. This was one of those situations.

He lowered his head, scowled at her and she started blabbering. "I didn't paint any of... I mean, I didn't know.... They told me it was okay....I didn't think...my mom is gonna kill me!" Desmond lowered his voice and said, "Young lady, unless you tell me everything that's happening here, I'll be forced to take you downtown and you'll be in a whole mess of trouble."

Desmond couldn't write it all down as fast as Martha was spewing it out. In a nutshell, she had a so-called boyfriend who had some painter friends of his from Florida painting these reproductions. He would drive down, pick them up, Martha would sell them and they'd all split the money. Nobody got hurt. Except the buyers who thought they were purchasing an original Becca Bernstein or Kadar Brock, when in fact they were purchasing a well done facsimile from a beach bum in Boca Raton.

After making Martha squirm and sweat for another thirty minutes, he finally told her (ordered her) to take down and destroy all the remaining paintings. He wanted names and addresses of all those who purchased previous paintings as well. Martha started whimpering. Then she really started crying.

She was finally able to tell Desmond that all the paintings in question were only sold in cash. That was one reason the buyers were able to get such "special" deals, because it was all done in cash. No records were kept, no names were taken.

Desmond told her he'd be back tomorrow to check and make sure all these paintings had been destroyed. He then told her if she took the money left from the sale of these forgeries and donated it to the Children's Home immediately, (like today), the judge might go easy on her. He scared her some more until he was pretty sure she wet her pants. Then he told her he'd be back to check on things.

He went back to his office, changed his clothes, took off his hairpiece and went back to Skippy's Hot Dogs, which was next door to the gallery, and ordered two hot dogs, all the way, with fries and a Dr. Pepper. He sat inside and watched as a van soon pulled up in front of the gallery and two Hispanic guys started loading the paintings into the truck. When the truck pulled away, Desmond strolled by the gallery window, casually glancing inside at four bare walls and Martha sitting at the counter sobbing.

He took out his cell phone and called Abbey. When he answered, Desmond said, "She's leaving home." And he closed the call. Abbey didn't need to answer. He smiled, knowing he had surreptitiously helped the only woman he had ever loved.

Chapter 39

THE WORK WEEK CAME TO AN END, Martha and her nonsense had been dealt with and unfortunately there would be no opportunity to see Harpreet in her running shorts on Saturday. So, he decided to drive back up to Harrah's Cherokee Casino and play some poker. He arrived about 10:00 Friday night and decided to let poker determine how long he stayed.

 He went directly to the high stakes room and bought $15,000 worth of chips. He didn't recognize any of the players there except for his old friend Mr. Wong. In a slight English accent, Mr. Wong said, "It's good to see you again my friend, did you bring enough chips to stay a while?" Abbey smiled at him and replied, " If I didn't bring enough chips with me, I'm sure you'll let me use some of yours ….won't you?" Wong didn't reply, he simply nodded with an expression on his face that was half way between a sneer and scowl. Abbey thought to himself, "Be careful!"

 He started slowly again, trying to "read" each of the other players. He already knew Wong. Just as he thought, Wong began bullying all the other players, making huge bets, forcing them to routinely fold their hands to him. He knew Wong could not have the best hand EVERY time. That's not possible. In fact, it's very hard to make a pair in poker. He knew Wong was just intimidating the others into submission.

Abbey sat next to an older black man who had retired from Philip Morris Tobacco Co. several years ago, and a pot-bellied middle-aged man who was wearing a 70's leisure suit. Abbey wondered where in the world he got that suit from, while silently hoping that style never came back. Each time Wong bet large, the older black man, whose name was Bobby, and the leisure suit guy, whose name was Luke, would fold.

They were each grumbling to anyone who would listen, including Abbey, about how good Wong was running. Every time they had a good hand, he seemed to have a better hand. They couldn't understand it. Abbey asked Bobby how he knew Wong always had a better hand. Bobby said, "Because every time I bet, he re-raises me by a large amount. He has to have something good." Luke said the same thing, "Yeah, he does that to me too, he's always getting the nuts."

Abbey looked at Bobby, then at Luke, and said, "When you fold, do you ever see his cards?" "Well, no, he never shows them, but he has to have something to be betting that big." Abbey did not want to tell anyone how to play, or not play. They were big boys and it was their money. If they wanted to donate it to Wong, that was their choice. They could always get up and walk away.

Unless Abbey had very good cards, he folded, or else only played hands when Wong folded. The other players were as easy to read as a James Patterson novel. He slowly built his chips at the expense of everyone else. A couple of hands, after Wong had folded, Abbey didn't even look at the cards that were dealt to him. Instead, he looked around at the other players, then made a substantial bet. Each time he did this, all the others folded. He was building a reputation.

However, sooner or later, the two table bullies had to confront each other. It was inevitable. He knew when that hand happened, Wong would most assuredly bet him all-in. At this point in the night, he had won $4,144. Not a large amount, but he certainly didn't want to donate it to Wong.

Then, THAT HAND, happened. THAT HAND is always the one where you have the best hand, but your opponent "thinks" he has the best hand. Abbey was dealt a 9 and 10 of spades. Wong was dealt the ace and king of spades. Wong bet a healthy amount, Abbey then called the bet, hoping for some luck on the flop. He got it.

The three flop cards were the 6, 7 and 8 of spades, giving each man a flush. Wong thought he had the nut flush, with the Ace high. Unfortunately for him, Abbey now had a straight flush, 6 through 10—an unbeatable hand in any poker match. A very, very slight tremble in Wong's eyelid told him that Wong had also hit the flush and "thought" he now had the best hand. Abbey was now akin to a good strong tree limb, all he had to do was give Wong enough rope. Gravity would do the rest.

Wong bet $5,000 on the next card and Abbey immediately called that bet. When the last inconsequential card was dealt, Wong looked at him and said, "I'm glad you brought a large stack of chips to the table my friend. Now, I want them." He looked at the dealer and said, "All-in."

Abbey didn't hesitate and pushed all his $19,144 of chips into the middle. He then looked up at Wong and quoted an old Chinese proverb, "Some people learn by Reading. Others learn by Observation. The rest of us have to pee on the electric fence."

When Wong saw he was beaten by Abbey's straight flush, he was rigidly still for nearly ten seconds. Then he looked directly at Abbey and said about ten words in Chinese, which Abbey was pretty sure were all curse words, then got up from the table and walked away.

Abbey may have looked calm to all the remaining players, but his insides were exploding with excitement. He played a few more meaningless hands. It was apparent no one left at the table was brave enough to stay in a hand with him. Finally, he rose from the table, flipped the dealer a $100 chip and walked towards the nearest bar.

He ordered his regular bar drink, an Iron Maiden, and sat there trying to unwind while listening to the constant jingles and jangles from the slot machines. He was thinking of ordering a second Iron Maiden when someone walked up behind him and spoke. It was Wong, asking if he could sit down at his table.

Abbey nodded and the two men sat staring at each other for a few moments before Wong spoke. He said, "You're very lucky my friend. Have you always been this way?"

"Not really, you always seem to bring it out in me." Abbey's inner voice starting screaming at him, "BE CAREFUL ABHINANDAN—-BE CAREFUL!"

Wong rose from the table, looked down at him and said, "Have a safe trip back to Winston-Salem." He walked away without another word.

The thought of playing cards again with Mr. Wong was not high on his priority list Saturday morning. He wasn't comfortable knowing that Wong took enough of an interest in him to find out where he lived. In fact, it was a little spooky. He spent a restless night, dreaming of running shorts and blonde hair. He thought to himself, "I used to be the one in control of my decisions with women. Now, I'm completely lost and have no determination whatsoever in my love life. I'm a loser. I'm pitiful!"

He decided he'd go back home after he had something to eat. He went to the restaurant at the hotel and ordered the "Appalachian Breakfast" which was three eggs, four pieces of bacon, two large pancakes, grits and three biscuits with jelly. He looked at the mountain of food in front of him and thought, "There is no way in the world a human being can eat all this food!" Then, he ate it all.

He arrived back home to find two email messages, one from his grandfather and one from Desmond Jones. His grandfather always came first, his message read,

"IF YOU LEND SOMEONE $20 AND NEVER SEE THAT PERSON AGAIN, IT WAS PROBABLY WORTH IT."

Okay….I understand that.

The other message from Desmond Jones read, "Call me as soon as you get this message Chief."

When Abbey got back home, he looked up the number and called him. Desmond answered and Abbey said, "What's wrong? And, I'm not a chief."

Desmond replied, "So, you're just one of the little 'worker bee' Indians?" Abbey disgustedly said, "What's wrong?"

"It seems your little girlfriend has closed the gallery, cleaned out her apartment and left town."

Abbey said, "I told you she's not my girlfriend and I don't see anything wrong with that."

"I didn't say anything was wrong Tonto, I only told you to call me. I thought you might be interested. That's all."

Abbey thought hard, but couldn't think of something clever to come back with. He finally said, "Okay, let me know if you hear anything else."

"Will do, Crazy Horse." But before he hung up, Abbey suddenly remembered something and said, "Wait! I need you to do something for me. I'll be down to your office in fifteen minutes."

"It's Saturday Red Cloud, I'm at home."

Abbey said, "Give me your address, I need you to do something for me. It's easy and quick and you'll like it. Trust me." He punched in the address in his GPS and drove to a small street in the West End called Blue Jay Way, where he found Desmond's house. There were two cars in the driveway and a very attractive Latina woman, in a short skirt, sweeping off the front porch when he pulled in.

He walked up the steps to the porch and she said, "He's inside, go on in." He went in the front door and Desmond had his feet propped up, watching an Irish rugby league match on TV. Abbey looked at him and asked, "Is that your wife out there?"

"Wife? I don't need no wife when I've got her." Abbey asked, "Girlfriend?" Desmond leaned over close to him, lowered his voice and said, "She's illegal. I found out about her and her family and I'm blackmailing them all. She cleans my house, cooks all my meals and gives me sex anytime I want it."

Abbey's mouth actually dropped open. He couldn't believe what he'd just heard. He said, "Really?"

Desmond answered, "No numnuts, she's from a cleaning service. I thought you Indians were supposed to be smart."

After collecting himself Abbey told him what he wanted. Take an envelope down to the restaurant where Annie Norwood worked and make sure she got it—anonymously. For his trouble, Abbey would buy his lunch at the restaurant and pay him $100. Desmond said, "Forget the money, just buy me and her lunch." Abbey agreed. The envelope had $711 in it.

They shook hands and Abbey walked out the door. He stopped and looked at the young cleaning lady on the porch and said, "I don't know how you can take it." She winked and said, "The same way you do." He shook his head, got in the car and drove away.

Chapter 40

IT WAS RAINING SUNDAY MORNING and he wasn't sure if Mrs. Carter would go to church in such messy weather. But she was there, waiting on him inside the front door of the church. Before he could say hello, or anything else, she scolded him by saying, "What did you do to Harpreet?"

"I didn't do anything to Harpreet. What are you talking about?"

Mrs. Carter said, "Well, I asked her to sit with us and she said, 'I don't think your friend wants me around.' Why would she say that? You didn't hurt her feelings did you Abhinandan?"

"I told you Mrs. Carter, I didn't do anything to her. You know how women are." As soon as he said this, he knew it was a mistake. She looked up at him and opened her mouth, but no sound came out. She finally said something that sounded like, "Hmmph!" He followed her in and they started singing "How Great Thou Art" with the choir.

During the other hymns and the announcements and the offering, she kept looking over at him and making that same sound, "Hmmph!" Things returned to normal, however, when she fell asleep on his shoulder during the sermon.

He didn't see Harpreet during church, nor afterwards. When he walked Mrs. Carter out, she turned to face him and solemnly said, "Abhinandan, what you're looking for isn't out there...it's in you." Which was eerily similar to the last email he read from his grandfather this morning,

"ABHINANDAN, YOU'RE NOT WHO YOU THINK YOU ARE, BUT WHO YOU THINK YOU ARE."

When he read the message from his grandfather this morning before church, he didn't understand the meaning. He did now.

He left Mrs. Carter and started walking towards the parking lot. He was still thinking about her statement to him and didn't notice someone standing at his car waiting on him—Harpreet. He slowed his pace and when he came near her he hesitantly said, "Good morning." (Almost as if it was a question.) Ten seconds of silence, then Harpreet said, "There's a concert at Salem College tonight, do you want to go with me?"

Abbey asked, "Who's playing?"

"Does it matter?"

"No, what time should I pick you up?"

She said, "I'll just meet you there. It starts at 7:00. Don't be late." She turned and walked away without another word. He had two thoughts: "Wow!" and, "Boy, she really does know how to walk."

The concert at Salem College was a performance by Leon Russell. Abbey thought he had died during the 70's or 80's. The concert was part country, part folk , part rock, part hillbilly and totally weird. Not the performance, but sitting next to Harpreet, with neither of them not knowing quite what to say to each other.

When the show ended and they walked outside, he asked her, "Would you like to go somewhere for a drink?" She quickly replied, "No." Then she said, "Thank you for coming tonight." She turned to walk away, took two steps, then turned back towards him and said, "You can call me sometime if you want to." Then she did walk away.

Monday morning he deposited some more money from his poker winnings in Mrs. Carter's account. She was in good shape. He checked Annie Norwood's bank account, which took about five seconds, she had less than $200 in it. The cost of the medicine for her son kept her living at, or below, the poverty level each month. He may have to increase his giving to her. Even with his gifts to Annie and Mrs. Carter, the money he won at cards was paying all his expenses, without having to use any of his salary.

His only real indulgence was clothes. He enjoyed nice suits, custom shoes and accessories. When he moved to Winston-Salem and started work he bought a new Audi. He was certain he'd get a BMW or Mercedes, but when he test drove the Audi, his mind was made up. He loved it. He upgraded his personal computer equipment as well. Not by buying new hardware, but by buying new parts and designing his own equipment. He wanted things that weren't sold in stores. In fact, the things he designed for himself hadn't been invented yet, by anyone else.

He continued to impress and amaze those at Lonewolf and at Baptist Hospital and Forsyth Medical Center. He was a star and a hot commodity. The articles in the local paper and the Winston-Salem Magazine had made everyone in the technological field aware of his presence. Wake Forest made overtures to him about doing some consulting work and specialty training for their staff. He wasn't interested. He wasn't concerned in teaching people about what was already out there. He wanted to explore what wasn't out there.

He went to Finnegan's after work two or three times each week, not for the food per se, but for the atmosphere and to spend a few moments with his friend Opie. One evening he walked in and took his usual seat at a small table near the foosball machine. Opie brought him a Guinness over, before he even ordered it. Opie said, "What's new my friend? And why don't you ever have a date?"

Abbey replied, "I can't find a date because all the girls are chasing you."

Opie laughed and asked, "Why didn't the toilet paper cross the road?" Before Abbey could respond, he said, "Because it got stuck in a crack." And they both laughed. He asked Abbey about his work and about any women he might be interested in. Then he asked him why his computer was so slow and why it kept locking up. And finally asked him if he thought the new waitress he just hired had a nice looking butt.

Abbey tried to answer each question as diplomatically as possible, under the circumstances, (the new waitress did indeed have a nice looking butt). Then Opie said, "I'm thinking of opening a small winery with my friend Josh. Would you want to be a partner in it? I think we can get some financing from the city to build it downtown, it wouldn't take a whole lot to get it started."

This really surprised Abbey, he didn't know how to respond. He said, "Get me any information you can and what sort of capital investment it would take, and I'll look at it. It sounds interesting." Opie said, "I may sound goofy sometimes, but I know what I'm doing. I'm a smart businessman. I wouldn't do this if I didn't think it would work."

Abbey knew he was telling the truth. The restaurant business is tough and Opie's place was very successful. He told Opie, "I know you are and I'm interested. Get me some information and we'll talk." His mind was now buzzing with thoughts of wineries and of Harpreet. Now, if he could only somehow suppress the ever-present , lingering , dominating thoughts of Juliette from his mind, he might find peace.

Chapter 41

THE NEXT WEDNESDAY, AFTER WORK, he was sitting in his condo staring into a small fire he had burning. He was thinking of a project he was formulating that surprised him and he was trying to collate those thoughts in his mind. He was also thinking of Harpreet. The phone rang and startled him. He had visions of long legs in running shorts jogging down 4th Street in his mind. He answered the phone and it was Gloria, Mrs. Carter's granddaughter.

She told him Mrs. Carter's husband had peacefully passed away that morning. It wasn't a surprise, but death is never truly unforeseen either. She said her grandmother was taking it as well as could be expected and she specifically asked Gloria to call him and give him the details and arrangements.

This news made him concerned for Mrs. Carter and how she would handle it. It also made him think about his own grandfather. How would he ever adjust to losing him? He opened his laptop and quickly wrote a note to his grandfather telling him how much he missed him. He also told him how much he loved him and how much his correspondence meant to him.

Within ten minutes his grandfather wrote back,

"WHO DIED?"

"How did you know someone died Grandfather?"

"BECAUSE YOU ARE NEVER IN THAT TYPE OF MOOD. WAS IT SOMEONE CLOSE TO YOU?"

He told him about Mrs. Carter and her husband and several other things going on in his life. He did not mention Harpreet. He told him that he never really thought of death much, young people seldom do. But this news caused him to think of those close to him, like his grandfather, his parents, even Mrs. Carter. His grandfather wrote back,

"ABHINANDAN, THE FEAR OF DEATH FOLLOWS FROM THE FEAR OF LIFE. A MAN WHO LIVES FULLY IS PREPARED TO DIE AT ANY TIME."

The funeral was Saturday morning at the church where Mr. and Mrs. Carter were married and were members for 70 years. All Mrs. Carter's family was there, as were most church members, including Harpreet. The service opened with one of Mrs. Carter's sons going to the pulpit to read something he had copied from an old Auden poem. He changed it somewhat to fit the occasion.

"Stop all the clocks, cut off your cell phone,

Prevent the dog from barking with a juicy bone.

Silence the pianos and with muffled drum

Bring out the coffin, let the mourners come.

Let the airplanes circle moaning overhead

Scribbling on the sky the message He Is Dead,

Put crepe bows round the white necks of the public doves,

Let the traffic policemen wear black cotton gloves.

He was our North, our South, our East and West,

Our morning week and our Sunday rest,

Our noon, our midnight, our talk, our song;

We thought his love would last forever: We were wrong.

Pack up the moon and dismantle the sun;

Pour away the ocean and sweep up the crumbs.

For now nothing good shall ever come."

When the family filed out of the church, Mrs. Carter saw him standing in a pew near the back. She stopped and went over to him and wrapped her arms around him and didn't let go. She wasn't crying, but she couldn't speak either. She didn't need to. She hugged him and he hugged her back. Everyone else stopped and waited. When she finished, she looked up at him, still unable to speak. He nodded at her, and smiled. Then, she went to bury her husband.

He stood and watched them leave for the private ceremony at the graveyard in God's Acre. His mind and thoughts were with Mrs. Carter, he didn't notice Harpreet walk up beside him. She didn't say anything until he became aware of the fragrance she was wearing and turned towards her. "It was a beautiful ceremony, I'm sure Mrs. Carter appreciated you coming."

He didn't turn to look at her, he just said, "Yes, it was a beautiful ceremony, for a beautiful woman." Then he turned to face Harpreet and asked, "Would you like to go out to dinner with me tonight?" She paused a few seconds and said, "No," then continued, "but I'd like to cook you dinner at my house, if you're interested." He quickly answered, "Yes, I'm interested. What time should I be there?" She said, "7:00…" and before she could finish her sentence, he finished it for her by saying, "And I won't be late."

Harpreet lived in a condo at the other end of 4th Street from him. He walked the six blocks passing the now familiar places he liked to visit: Mellow Mushroom, Camino's, The Steven's Center, Hutch & Harris, Skippy's Hot Dogs, Foothills Brewery, The Filling Station and Mozelles. He brought a bottle of Chardonnay with him, assuming that Harpreet (like most women) would like it. He also assumed she drank wine. She didn't.

Additionally, he assumed she might be dressed in traditional Indian attire, and again his assumptions were off base. She wore an ankle length dress, with a slit up the side all the way to mid-thigh, which flaunted one of her most appealing assets. His final mis-assumption was that it might be an awkward evening, given their recent history. He was very wrong.

Harpreet wasn't vegetarian, but had prepared a vegetarian meal that he found incredible. He was a meat eater, but this dinner left him very well pleased and surprised that he actually enjoyed it so much. After dinner, they sat at the bay window, overlooking the traffic on 4th Street. Not the most stimulating of views, but somehow calming and relaxing.

There were seldom any topics of conversation they agreed on, but they didn't argue either. Each listened to the other explain their own points of view on race relations, world politics, music, history, arts and travel. Harpreet was probably a little more rounded in her experiences and cultural awarenesses than he was, but she didn't try to expose any deficiencies he showed. They talked and they listened to each other. She would cross her legs and the slit in her dress seemed to grow proportionately to the excitement of the conversation. Or, maybe that was just his excitement that was growing. He was unsure.

He was unclear if she was aware of the moving slit in her dress, or not. She was aware. What she was unaware of was if he was noticing the slit in her dress or not. He was. He didn't wear a watch because he prided himself on being able to tell what the time was without a watch. He thought it was probably about 10:15 or 10:30. He would have bet money on it. It had started to rain during the night and Harpreet said, "I'm not sure if any taxis run this late, you didn't bring an umbrella did you?"

He said, "What time is it?" "1:20," she replied. He couldn't believe it. He lied to her and said that he had left his umbrella down in the lobby. She knew it was a lie, but decided to let him save face and get away with it. He apologized for staying so long. She truthfully said she enjoyed it. He walked to the door with her and opened it, he looked back at her and she said, "I'm not going to kiss you Abbey. It doesn't feel right. Maybe it will in the future, but tonight it doesn't. Do you understand?"

Well…there were about a dozen or so responses to this question. None of them were going to make either of them comfortable. So, he took the easiest path available and simply said, "Yes." He started walking home in the rain. When he crossed the street from her building, he was tempted to look up at her window to see if she was looking back at him. If she was indeed looking at him, then that would be a good sign. If she wasn't, well, that wouldn't be too good. He slowed, stopped, thought of turning to look back, then chickened out and kept on walking.

Chapter 42

HE DIDN'T THINK MRS. CARTER would be at church Sunday morning. He was wrong. She was in her usual pew waiting on him. He came in and sat beside her, putting his arm around her shoulders. She looked up at him and said, "I wish I could've told him I loved him one more time before he passed away." He smiled back at her and replied, "He knew that, Mrs. Carter, he knew. You just have to have faith that everything will turn out okay." She took his hand and replied, "No son, faith is about being okay no matter how things turn out."

He decided to make the drive up to Stone Mountain Sunday afternoon. He needed some time for reflection on the events of the past week. Only two cars were in the lower parking lot, which was a good sign for him. He took his little pack with some water, nuts, cheese and an orange and started up the side of the mountain, not on the main trail that had steps. He wanted a route that wasn't a trail. One that was steep and dangerous that went straight up the bald face of the old mountain. As he started his climb, one of the other tourists called out to him, "Hey, you can't do that, you'll fall." Abbey looked at him and replied, "And who would care, sir? Just who would care if I fell?"

He made it to the top without falling and without breaking a sweat—barely. He found it as he'd left it before, as it had been for the last six thousand years: bare, naked, windswept, lonely and beautiful. He found a place in the sun, with a boulder to lean back against and watched the buzzards soaring above and below him. Certainly, they were always on the lookout for a meal, but more assuredly they were simply enjoying the life God had granted them. Floating above the cruel world, taking advantage of the ever-present thermals from the mountain. Never having to flap those long, silver-tipped wings. Riding with the wind, not a worry in the world. Always confident dinner would be waiting for them...always waiting for them.

He sat up there all alone and contemplated life. He also contemplated death. He thought of a timetable for the sun's demise. Then he thought of her smile and her eyes. He thought of love. And love lost. And the hope of love to come. He became mired in his dreams and lost all concept of time that day, which was unusual for him. He believed that a man could never find, or need, better companionship than that of himself. Then he remembered Juliette. He remembered their talks. He remembered the time spent alone with her when conversation wasn't needed. He remembered everything. How she made him feel like no other woman had ever made him feel. The only thing he couldn't solve that day was how to stop thinking about her.

When he returned home that evening, he was comforted to find a message from his grandfather,

"ONE DAY YOU WILL WAKE UP AND REALIZE THERE ISN'T ANY MORE TIME LEFT TO DO THE THINGS YOU'VE ALWAYS WANTED . DO IT NOW."

But he thought, "How can I do the things I want to do? Now that she's married."

236

Work was a grind the next week. He had to attend a couple of functions set up by Novant Health celebrating a new contract with Lonewolf. These things were usually boring and he hated having to make "small talk" with the executives who had no idea what he actually did. The second function took place at Pine Brook Country Club, because Lonewolf's president thought it would make Abbey happy.

He felt uneasy about meeting Robyn Warren again, especially since he'd been ignoring her emails and phone calls ever since that fateful night together. He was hoping she had gotten the message and had moved on to other prey. He was wrong. She immediately spotted him and clung to him as though attached by Velcro. She laughed at everything he said and unnecessarily promoted him to all the other guests. She stood as close as she could to him and kept turning and rubbing her body against his. It was almost claustrophobic for him.

The only peace he could find was in visiting the men's room, not because he had to go, but simply to get away. One of the club attendants at the party happened to be in there as well, washing his hands when he walked in. Abbey said, "Pardon me sir, can I ask you to do me a huge favor?" Of course the guy would've done anything any of the guests asked him to, and answered, "Certainly sir, what do you need?"

Abbey asked him if he had a cell phone with him, the guy did, so he gave him his number and told him to call that number in about three minutes. The attendant asked, "What do you want me say?" He didn't want him to say anything. "Just call the number and hang up when I answer." "Yes sir, anything you say." As he was thinking to himself, "These rich guys sure are crazy."

He went back out and instantly Robyn was attached to his side again, smiling and rubbing against him. Then, his phone rang. He reached inside his coat pocket, answered the phone and said, "Yes….yes…I understand. Can it wait? Of course, I'm on my way." He looked at Robyn and said an "emergency" had come up and he had to leave, he asked her if she would please make his apologies to everyone. Her smile quickly turned into a look of despair. She said, "Of course I will. Call me later. Do you still have my number?"

He didn't want to lie to her, so he said, "Yes, I do have your number. Got to run, bye." And he quickly walked out. Well, technically, he did have her number somewhere in his deleted phone message file. And he didn't say he WOULD call her back. So, no harm, no foul. Now all he had to do was avoid her this weekend, because he was certain she'd be calling him, or worse, come over to his place again unannounced.

Between Wednesday night and Friday afternoon, he had four emails, two phone mail messages and umpteen unanswered phone calls from Robyn. He packed a small case Friday morning and left from work early for Cherokee.

Mrs. Carter wouldn't need the $9,000 each month now for nursing home expenses, but he still wanted to supplement her bank account (and Annie Norwood's) to make sure they were comfortable. This enabled him to stay away from the high stakes room, and Mr. Wong, and just play at the regular tables. Sometimes he felt guilty about winning so often. His opponents were just weekend players who tried to bluff him with sweat popping out on their upper lips. Or, they would try to smooth play a pair of Aces when their faces were flushed red, or their eyes were dilated. All too frequently, it was becoming too easy for him.

He didn't see Wong Friday night and that was a relief. He played with all the truck drivers, car salesmen, retirees and wannabes until one-by-one, none of them would play with him any longer. It was no fun for them losing constantly to this well dressed foreigner. He called it a night around 11:00 and decided to have an Iron Maiden before going to his room. He'd won $1,371.

He sat at a corner table to watch the people pass by and was waiting for the waitress to come over and take his order. When she did come, she already had his drink, an Iron Maiden, and said, "It's from him." Pointing to the bar where Wong sat smiling at him. "Oh crap!" He was thinking maybe Robyn Warren would have been a better alternative after all.

Wong came over and sat down across from him without asking if he could sit down. "I see you enjoy playing with the little people and taking their money." Abbey was silently thinking to himself, "Be careful Abhinandan." He finally couldn't help himself any longer and said, "I don't really take their money as much as they give it to me…similar to you." And his inner voice screamed, "ARE YOU CRAZY?"

Wong didn't say anything but Abbey was sure his grip was going to shatter the drink glass he was holding. Wong rose, looked down at him and said, "Enjoy your stay." He walked up to the bar and slammed his glass down, spilling the contents on a Lumbee Indian from Pembroke. He apologized, paid the man's bar tab and walked away.

Chapter 43

HE ROSE SATURDAY MORNING and checked his email before breakfast. He was relieved to find a message from his grandfather,

"MISERY IS A GIFT FROM GOD TO SHOW YOU YOU'RE SEARCHING FOR 'THINGS' IN ALL THE WRONG PLACES."

After suitably reflecting on this missive he picked up his cell phone and called Desmond Jones. He answered on the fourth ring, not with a "Hello," but with "What now?" Abbey answered, "I need you to check out something, or rather, someone for me. Can you do that?"

"Look Maharishi, it's Saturday. Don't things ever happen to you Monday through Friday?"

"I'm sorry, but I need to find some information pretty quickly. You can probably do it from your house in an hour or two and you know I'll make it worth your effort."

"An hour or two? So now you know my job and how long things will take do you? Well, I'm getting ready to go take a dump. How long is that going to take me?"

"Okay Desmond, I'm sorry again. But I'm out of town and I need some information pretty quickly. Can you help me?"

"Alright Dalai Lama, what do you need?"

"I'm pretty sure the Dalai Lama isn't Indian."

"If you want this crap done today, he's Indian."

"You're right, I think he is Indian. I want you to check out a man named Win Wong, or Wong Win; I'm not really sure which is his first name. I think he lives near Cherokee, he's always at the casino here. I need to know his story, or as much as you can find out about him. Okay?"

He had already looked online at Wong, but since he wasn't sure of his correct name and didn't know where he banked or even where he lived, it was a fruitless search. If he'd been home, with his all his equipment, he would have been more successful, but all he had with him was a small tablet. That's why he was hoping Desmond Jones could help him.

Desmond asked him, "Why are you in Cherokee? Are you gambling? And, finally, are you in trouble?"

Abbey replied, "None of your business. None of your business. And, I hope not. That's why I need your help. Call me back as soon as you know something. And Desmond, I need this information quickly."

"Just sit tight and strum your sitar Ravi, I'll get back with you."

He decided he'd go down to the little café in the hotel and have a cup of coffee. Thoughts of Wong had curbed his appetite. He was seated and a young waitress came to his table, smiled and said, "What can I get for you?" Abbey said, "Coffee please." She blushed a little and started reading, "We have Caffe Latte, Caffe Mocha, White Chocolate Mocha, Cinnamon Dolce Latte, Skinny Vanilla Latte, Caramel Macchiato, Caramel Flan Latte, Iced Coffee, Mocha, Iced Caramel Mocha and Evolution Fresh Grande. Which would you like?"

His grandfather told him once, "BE NICE, IT DOESN'T COST YOU ANYTHING."

He smiled at her again and said, "Black please, maybe a little cream." He sipped his coffee and stared at his cell phone, both were disappointing him. He went to the small gym at the hotel and walked on the treadmill a little, very little. He decided he'd play a few quarters in the slot machines and had lost about $10 when his phone rang.

Abbey answered, "Hello." Desmond responded, "Abhinandan, stay away from him. Do not mess with him, do not cross him, don't even say hello to him. Do you understand me?"

Not the answer he was hoping for. "Tell me what you mean Desmond."

"I mean stay the crap away from him, he's dangerous. Very dangerous."

"Why do you say he's dangerous, who told you that?"

"Look numnuts, I know people. I know some people who know people at the casino up there. All I had to do was mention his name and they started shaking. Apparently, he'd been a big deal up at Atlantic City and had a run in with some guy who then disappeared. I mean totally disappeared. He was asked to leave by some heavyweights and he ended up in Cherokee. Do not mess with him, do you understand me?"

Abbey took a deep breath and said, "It might be too late for that."

"What have you done? Get in your car and leave that place NOW! You do not want to get on the bad side of this guy. Leave now!"

He took another deep breath and said, "Okay, I will. Thanks for helping. I really appreciate it."

But he wasn't going to leave, not yet. He had a plan. He hoped it would work.

He walked down to the high stakes poker room and was relieved to not see Wong in there. Just as he figured, Wong probably played at night only. There was only one table in play and he took one of the two remaining seats. Again, he started out slowly, folding nearly every hand. The other players were pretty reckless with their bets and within thirty minutes he had a pretty good "read" on them.

The guy wearing a cowboy hat always bluffed, except when he actually had a hand, then he would slow play it. The young black guy wearing three necklaces, four rings, two bracelets, earrings and a nose ring actually knew what he was doing. He needed to watch him closely. The white guy with a Mohawk didn't have a clue and Abbey knew he'd lose all his money quickly. The final player was an older woman who didn't say anything to anyone, she just drank and played. She could have been 38 or 58. There was no way to tell without scrapping off the makeup.

Even though this was the high stakes poker table, the bets were usually pretty small, most pots averaging between $100 and $200. He began entering more pots when he was sure he had good reads, and most of the time, he was right. The white guy with the Mohawk gave up after losing a bundle in less than an hour. A middle-aged man wearing shorts that were too short and a sleeveless shirt that was too tight took the open seat. He didn't stay long either. He went all-in with only an Ace high, not even a pair. Abbey graciously accepted his money.

After several hours of play, with him and the bejeweled black guy staying out of each other's way, he decided he'd met his goal. As usual, he flipped the dealer a hundred dollar chip and walked away with $3,973. Not as much as he'd hoped for, but enough to ensure his plan would be successful, hopefully.

He went to the regular room that evening and sat in at a table playing small hands and folding as much as possible. However, he couldn't help himself and ended up winning anyway. He wasn't there to win, he was there to let Wong see him there and invite him over to the high stakes room to play with him. Eventually, Wong made his entrance, accompanied by an Asian beauty wearing either a mini-skirt or a wide belt. Abbey wasn't sure which it was.

He pretended not to notice Wong and played a few more hands when the predictable happened. A well dressed man tapped him on the shoulder and told him Mr. Wong had invited him to play at his table. He looked over at Wong, waited about ten seconds, then nodded.

Each man seemed to avoid playing any pots with the other. They were initially just content to take the other players' money. He grew his winnings to $5,137 without ever playing a hand with Wong. Then, he noticed it. That tell-tale sign Wong had when he actually had a good hand. This was what he was waiting for, a good hand for Wong so he could enter the pot and bet all his money and let Wong win it!

By letting Wong win all his money, he thought he'd be off Wong's watch list. The problem was that he was dealt a straight! How in the world could that happen? Wong opened up and bet and all the others folded as usual, except him. He looked over at Wong, then looked down at his winning cards, then looked back at Wong and said, "I'm all in." He pushed all his $5,137 worth of chips into the middle, knowing Wong would call him. He did.

Wong turned over three 7's and smiled smugly at him. It took a lot of will power on his part, because his straight had Wong beat, but he looked at Wong and said, "You win my friend." Wong laughed and slapped the table. He got up, looked back at Wong and said, "You're just too good for me sir, goodnight everyone." He was pretty sure he'd now have a safe drive down the mountain, back to Winston-Salem.

He got home late and tired, but he knew he'd sleep well. Before bed, he checked his emails: two more from Robyn Warren, which he deleted, and one from his grandfather, which helped him sleep,

"WHEN YOU LOSE, DON'T LOSE THE LESSON."

Chapter 44

JULIETTE AND HER FAMILY, SUCH AS IT WAS, returned from Hawaii after a couple weeks' vacation. It was miserable for Juliette. Each day her brother spent out on the beaches and each night he spent in the clubs. She was left to babysit mom who became best friends with every bartender at the resort. The more she drank, the more blatant her sexual overtones were to anyone who would pay her any attention—any age.

Finally, the last day came and Juliette could actually look forward to going home. Then, her mother became sick. Her arm had swollen a little and was hurting her. It got to the point where she couldn't carry her bags and could barely walk to the gate for their flight. During the long flight home she became ill and threw up several times and it was clear that it was more serious than a sore arm.

Juliette had the taxi take them to an emergency room near the airport, while her brother took their luggage home. The doctors examined her and determined that something poisonous had bitten Mrs. Gideon's arm. They stabilized her and sent some blood work out for evaluation. The doctor told Juliette her mother could go home, but that she needed to stay quiet and needed bed rest until the medicines could start to work.

Ten days later her mother was still in bed. Juliette had grave doubts that it was because of her illness. She only seemed sick when Juliette was in her bedroom, otherwise, she was eating well and Juliette was quite sure she was sneaking some wine bottles into her room.

One afternoon, she told her mother she was going out to the grocery store and to run some errands, that she'd be back in two or three hours. However, that wasn't exactly true. She only drove out the driveway and around the corner where she pulled over and parked. She waited about fifteen minutes then walked back to the house, quietly unlocking the door and creeping upstairs. Just as she suspected, her mother was walking around the den, wine glass in hand, talking on the phone in a very sultry voice to someone named Allen.

After a big dramatic scene from her mother, Juliette simply said, "You're fine. I'm going back to Winston-Salem as soon as I can make arrangements. And by that, I mean tomorrow!" Her mother cried and pleaded as Juliette silently began packing her things. She was going home and there was nothing her mother could do, nor any type of tantrum or threat she could use that could keep Juliette there one more day.

Juliette arrived at her home in Ardmore late at night. She stayed up all night cleaning, reading junk mail and sorting out her life. She knew the gallery was closed. Martha told her she had "personal issues" to resolve and had moved away. Juliette still paid the rent and the utilities, and it would be a relatively simple matter to open it back up. Her dad's life insurance policies had left her and her brother in excellent financial shape. She didn't need her mother's help any longer.

The following day, Juliette called some friends from the School of the Arts to let them know she was home and learned that Ian had moved away. They think he may have moved to Charlotte or Atlanta, but no one was really sure. No one really cared. She wondered how she had let someone like him almost ruin her life. But she was home now. She'd open the gallery again and hopefully her life would be back to normal. However, she wondered if Abbey would ever be a part of it again?

Chapter 45

THE PHONE WOKE HIM EARLY SUNDAY MORNING, it was Desmond Jones calling. Without saying hello, Abbey answered, "Are you worried about me paying you?"

"No, Kubla Khan, you'll pay me alright. I just wanted to make sure you weren't dead."

"I'm fine. Everything is good now. I appreciate your help, now let me go back to sleep."

"If you keep messing around with people like Wong, you'll be asleep permanently, Mukherjee."

Abbey paused a moment and said, "Who?"

Desmond had him now, "Mukherjee, numnuts, he's the president of your country, India!"

"He's not my president. Remember, I'm American, just like you."

"Okay Cochise, don't get your little Indian panties in a wad. Go on back to sleep."

He thought of a really good come back, but Desmond had already hung up the phone…dang!

He did go back to sleep, however, and completely missed church. About 12:30 his phone rang again, he was hoping it was Desmond, he was saving his great comeback. It was Mrs. Carter. "Are you okay son, you're not sick are you? Do you want me to have Gloria bring you anything?"

"No ma'am, I'm fine. I just had a late night and overslept. Thanks for calling though."

"Hot date, huh? Harpreet?

"No ma'am, not Harpreet, nor anyone. Just a late night."

Not five minutes after Mrs. Carter's call, Harpreet called him. "Are you okay?"

"Yes, I'm fine, I just had a late night."

"It's not because of anything I said last week is it?"

It took him a moment or two to remember. She must be referring to the comment she made about not kissing him at the doorway. "No, certainly not. Look, would you like to have a late lunch with me?"

Pause…. Pause….Pause…. "Okay, where? Not hamburgers though."

Dang, he really wanted a Blarney Burger. "Sure, how about The Filling Station in about 45 minutes?"

Lunch was great, he had prime rib and Harpreet ordered a pasta salad with unsweetened iced tea. The conversation was easy, the awkwardness had ended and they felt a comfort with each other that hadn't been there before. It was unsaid at the time, but they both knew it was inevitable. They were becoming "friends."

They got together for casual dinners twice that week, as friends would. They both enjoyed it, but they each knew they must address the situation at some point soon. After dinner one night they decided to stop at Foothills, where a small jazz quartet was playing. He had a Salem Gold and Harpreet had an orange juice. During the intermission, Harpreet looked at him and said, "So, I understand you've got a thing for blondes."

"Well, I did have a thing for blondes, one blonde in particular. But that's over now. It's not that I'm….."

"Stop," she said, "I knew you did. You had a reputation at Virginia Tech. I checked."

"You checked on me? How did you do that? And why?"

"I have a friend there who'd do anything for me, he asked around and some people remembered you. You left quite an impression on the blonde, female population up there."

He looked at her and said, "But why were you asking?"

She tilted her head, hesitated, then finally answered, "Because I know I'm attractive, I know I have nice legs. I'm smart, successful and everything a man should be looking for. But you weren't. I figured you were already involved with someone, or you were a closet gay."

He looked at her, looked up at the ceiling, looked back at her, and she finally said, "Well?"

"I'm not gay. I thought that was obvious. I was involved with someone and it took me a long time to get over her. I'm not sure I'm over her yet. I can't believe you thought I was gay."

"Well, I went out of my way to run past you Saturday mornings. I spoke to you every Sunday at church. I was practically throwing myself at you and you didn't seem to notice, or care."

"Bad timing. The girl I was seeing suddenly left town, I was confused. I didn't know what had happened and it was hard, still is hard, getting over that."

"Why did she leave? Did you ever find out?"

"Yeah, she got married. Can you believe that? She flew home to California and got married."

He checked on Mrs. Carter's bank account, which was in good shape now that she didn't have the $9,000 a month bill from the nursing home. The balance in her account was very healthy because of her husband's life insurance policy, which added $250,000 to the total. He shouldn't have to be too concerned about her finances any longer. Annie Norwood was a different story. She could barely keep afloat, even with him helping. The cost of her son's medicines, doctor's visits and the time she had to miss from work taking care of him kept her near disaster.

He needed to make a substantial, anonymous gift to her. He called Desmond who answered the call, "What's wrong? Couldn't wait till the weekend to call me?"

"No, I couldn't. I need you to make another anonymous delivery for me to the girl at the restaurant where you went before. Can you do that today?"

"I can do it tonight, if she's working. I do have other clients besides you, Pocahontas."

"Wasn't Pocahontas a female?"

"What do you care? You're not even a real Indian! Drop the money off by the office after 6:00."

Abbey paused and said, "How do you know it's money?"

"Oh please, Red Cloud. Do you think I'm stupid? Of course it's money. I don't know what you did to this girl, and I don't care. But if you're the father, you should be paying her more!"

"I'm not the kid's father Desmond. Do you think I'M stupid? I'm just trying to help her out."

"Alright Hiawatha, don't scalp me. I was just checking. Be here after six, and you're buying me dinner!"

Chapter 46

HE WENT HOME, HAD A GLASS OF WINE and stared out towards the reticent, reserved monolith of Pilot Mountain. He still wished for answers from the all-knowing one, but even in its silence he felt more comfortable about things this evening. The latest email from his grandfather made him feel especially warm,

"TO MAKE A DIFFERENCE IN SOMEONE'S LIFE YOU DON'T HAVE TO BE BRILLIANT. OR, PERFECT. YOU JUST HAVE TO CARE."

He cared about Mrs. Carter, he cared about Harpreet, he cared about Annie Norwood, Opie and even old, crusty Desmond. He wished he could stop caring about someone else. But before blonde thoughts totally consumed his mind, the phone rang. He saw that it was from Desmond, so he answered it, "What now Sherlock?" He was very proud of himself and had been waiting several days to use that on Desmond.

After fifteen seconds of silence, Desmond said, "He's a policeman numnuts, I'm a private detective. I thought you were smarter than that."

"Well, he…"

"Shut up, I've got something to tell you. The girl, Annie, took your envelope, but said she wouldn't take any more money from you. She said she doesn't take handouts and that she's not a charity case. And, by the way, she knows who you are. She doesn't know your name, but she knows who you are."

"How could she know who I am? Did you tell her?"

"No, Humperdink, I didn't tell her. She said she remembered you from some protest she was at. Then she saw you again at her restaurant and you left a huge tip for her. She's not stupid, she figured it had to be you."

"Englebert Humperdink is not Indian. He's British. Are you sure you didn't tell her who I was?"

"No, I didn't tell her. And Humperdink was born in India, which is more than you can say."

Abbey thought a few seconds, then asked, "Is that all she said?"

"No Nehru, she wants to meet you."

"You've already used Nehru before."

"There's more than one Nehru numnuts. I thought you were Indian."

Abbey didn't know what to say. Finally, "Let me think about it. I'll call you back."

Desmond quickly replied, "Don't call back tonight. I'm having my house cleaned; if you know what I mean."

Abbey thought to himself, "There is no way under God's blue sky that I want to know what you mean." Instead, he only said, "Okay, goodnight."

He knew where Annie Norwood lived, so he went there after work and knocked on the door of her apartment. He knew she was home, he could hear the television in the background. She answered the door and stood looking at him, finally saying, "I knew it was you. Thank you for what you've done, but I don't take charity. I need the money obviously, and I'll gladly work for it, but I won't take charity."

She invited him inside the small, but tidy little apartment. Her son was lying in bed resting and watching TV. She gave him the overview of her life and her son's medical situation and apologized for the day at the picket line. The more she talked, the more he liked her.

All she'd ever done was waitressing and cleaning jobs, but had completed over two years of undergraduate work at Winston-Salem State University. She just couldn't afford to keep going. Her son's father left as soon as he found out she was pregnant. They were never married, in fact, love was never in the equation. She was content, and things were okay until her son's condition became worse requiring the expensive, experimental drugs. Her parents were from West Virginia and according to Annie, "In worse shape than I am." They couldn't help her.

He could. And he was. He just had to figure out how. He didn't need a housekeeper, his condo staff took care of those duties. He didn't need an assistant at work. Desmond didn't need an assistant and apparently had a housekeeper extraordinaire onboard already. But Mrs. Carter didn't.

He told Annie he needed to work on something, he asked her if she would be willing to be a "girl Friday" for an elderly woman he knew. That meant doing everything, including laundry, cooking, errands—everything. Annie looked towards her son's room and Abbey said "We can work that out as well." Now all he had to do was convince Mrs. Carter she did need someone and figure out how Annie's pay would work.

When he explained the whole idea to Mrs. Carter, she was silent for about sixty seconds, then she started crying. He thought to himself that he'd really screwed up now. Then, she said, "I think you've saved my life Abhinandan. I don't think I could take another week of Gloria's help. I know she's my granddaughter, and I love her, but she's about to drive me insane! I just have two questions: Is this Annie girl a Christian? And, do you trust her?"

He truly didn't know the answer to the first question, but he absolutely knew the answer to the second one, "Yes ma'am, to both questions. You'll love her." Mrs. Carter hugged him and cried some more while he was secretly hoping Annie Norwood wasn't a devil worshipper.

When he finally got back home, he was excited by all the events. He called Harpreet, but she was washing her hair and couldn't talk. He even called his parent's house but there was no answer. He was a little relieved at that. He finally wrote it all down and emailed it to his grandfather. Not asking for advice, just to be able to tell someone what was happening.

Shortly, he received the response,

"ABHINANDAN, I AM VERY PROUD OF YOU. IT'S NICE TO BE IMPORTANT, BUT IT'S MORE IMPORTANT TO BE NICE."

Chapter 47

MRS. CARTER AND ANNIE NORWOOD hit it off extremely well. Annie's son started calling Mrs. Carter "granny," at her request. He usually stayed at Mrs. Carter's house while Annie cleaned, cooked and ran errands. He amused Mrs. Carter as much as she amused him. Everything worked out well for everyone including Abbey. Now, he only had to win enough at poker to pay Annie's salary, instead of the rest home fees he was paying in the past.

Abbey had been avoiding one of his favorite places in town, Foothill's Brewery, because he would have to pass by Juliette's old gallery to get there. But, since Martha had closed the place up and left town, he could start visiting once again. He walked down 4th street, from his condo towards Foothill's, taking in all the sights and sounds of Winston and the Arts District. He liked the eclectic nature of the downtown area. When he crossed the street he noticed a light on in the gallery, which he thought was odd, since it had been dark since Martha left.

He was hoping Martha had not returned, so he stopped at the corner of the building and peeked inside the gallery just in case Martha was there. But, Martha was not there. Juliette was. He had to consciously make himself breathe to keep from passing out. Juliette had her hair pinned up and was painting one of the walls. She had on shorts and an old paint splattered shirt and he was quite convinced she was the most beautiful woman he'd ever seen.

He watched for about three minutes, it could've been longer, but he lost all concept of time. Finally, he backed away and wandered back towards his home. He forgot that he was hungry, he forgot he was thirsty, he almost forgot where he lived. He actually passed by his building about twenty feet before he came to his senses. Hundreds of questions were now flooding his mind. Why was she here? Where was her husband? Should I introduce myself to them? Is she going to re-open the gallery and live here? How did she get to be so beautiful? And, how am I going to be able to handle this? Seeing her with another man.

It was well past midnight before he went to bed, he couldn't stop his mind from racing. He rose early and read the overnight email from his grandfather,

"WE CAN IGNORE REALITY, BUT WE CANNOT IGNORE THE CONSEQUENCES OF IGNORING REALITY."

He wasn't entirely sure what this meant, but he felt that somehow the message was exactly meant for him at this precise moment in time. He waited till after 8:00 before calling Desmond. No answer. He called his cell phone, no answer there either. He left messages on them both hoping Desmond would call him back quickly. He wanted Desmond to find out what was going on at the gallery and also find out everything about Juliette and her husband.

Finally, after the eleventh phone message, Desmond called him back. When Abbey saw who the call was from, he didn't answer with "Hello," he said, "Where have you been? I need you!"

"Look Sanjay Gupta, I have other customers. Customers who pay a lot better than you and your cheap rupees."

Abbey was flustered and said, "Well, at least you could've answered some of my messages." Silence…silence…then Desmond replied, "Abhinandan, I work for who I want to work for. I only answer to me. You don't own me, or order me around. Do you understand that?"

"Yes, I'm sorry, it's just that something important came up and I need help. I really need you to check it out for me."

Desmond explained, "Is it more important than the wife of one of the leading businessmen in town running around with his fiercest competitor? And maybe spilling company secrets in their not-so-cozy love nest?"

Abbey thought for a moment and said, "Yes, it is. I don't care about some floozy running around on her husband. That means nothing to me."

"Well let me tell you something Chief Joseph, this floozy's husband will pay more for one day's work than I've made the entire time I've spent with you. Do you get the picture?"

"Do you do a lot of this type work? Catching husbands and wives running around on each other?"

"Look, Osceola, there's a place and time for everything. Actually, there aren't enough hours in the day to catch everyone who's cheating on their spouses. For me, it's job security. And these executives pay well to find out who their wives are sleeping with. The work I do for you is a welcome distraction for me, it's the only reason I've been helping you. Now, tell me what you want me to do before I change my mind and kick you off my reservation."

"You remember the art gallery that you went to before, the one that had the forged paintings? Well, it seems as though it's opening again. I saw the owner inside painting the walls. I heard she's opening it with her new husband and I want to find out if that's true and I want to know all about her and her husband. Find out anything and everything you can.

Desmond bit his lower lip and closed one eye before saying, "Why do you want to know this stuff? There's something you're not telling me."

"It doesn't matter why I want to know, I just do. Let me know what you find out as soon as you can."

He met Harpreet for dinner again Tuesday night at one of their favorite places, The Glass Onion. Their meetings were now free of pressure and the conversations were easy and comfortable. She was interested in why he couldn't seem to let go of Juliette's memory and why he wasn't able to adequately explain it. He tried to clarify his mixed feelings as best he could, but ignored her pleas to further describe who Juliette was exactly. He didn't think that was any of her business. She asked about Juliette's husband, and of course he had no idea. He didn't tell her he had a private investigator checking it out for him. He thought that might sound a little too weird.

He had to go to Charlotte for a business meeting Thursday and Friday, but he and Harpreet made plans to meet for breakfast at Camino's Saturday morning. He didn't hear back from Desmond until Friday and the wait was killing him. But he decided he wouldn't appear too over-anxious for the information.

When the call finally came through, he was driving back to Winston on I-85 and had to pull over at a rest stop. He was too nervous to drive and talk. Desmond opened with, "Well, you got your information wrong, that's what took me so long. I had to be sure."

"What information? Is she not opening the art gallery again?"

"Oh yeah, she's indeed going to open it again numnuts. But she's not married, never has been."

Abbey wasn't sure what he just heard. His mind didn't comprehend the words correctly. He was positive his mind was playing a trick on him. He asked Desmond to repeat that last piece of information.

"I said, she's NOT married numnuts. That's what you wanted to know isn't it? You don't care if some art gallery is opening or not, you only care about the hot blonde who owns it."

His mind didn't fool him, he had heard correctly. She's not married. She's really not married. What happened? Why isn't she married?

"Hey Sitting Bull….you still there?"

"Yeah, are you sure she's not married Desmond? I mean 100% sure??"

"Abhinandan, I can explain this to you again; but I can't comprehend it for you. I'm also going to pretend, for the sake of our friendship, that you're not questioning my integrity. However, I am going to charge you extra for insulting my professionalism. I'll mail you the bill. Bye."

He sat in his car holding his cell phone in front of him. He couldn't see anything or hear anything. He was totally incapable of driving at that moment. His mind was racing as fast as his heart was. How could she not be married? He didn't understand, but he was quite certain Desmond was thorough in his investigation. He had over an hour left to drive back to Winston. He wondered, "Who's going to drive my car?" He wasn't totally convinced he could.

Chapter 48

THE TRAFFIC FROM CHARLOTTE TO WINSTON-SALEM on I-85 was a usual horrible mess. 75 mph, stop. 70 mph, 20 mph, 55 mph, stop. Repeat this pattern over and over and throw in a handful of curse words. However, he had no recollection of the drive whatsoever. All he knew is that he pulled into his parking space alive and unwrecked. He poured a glass of wine, lit a fire and opened his emails. He didn't care about any of them except the one from his grandfather. Somehow he knew, he just knew, his grandfather would have a message for him that would stop his head from spinning. It did.

"JUST BECAUSE YOUR MIRACLE DIDN'T HAPPEN YESTERDAY DOESN'T MEAN IT CAN'T HAPPEN TODAY."

He woke early Saturday morning and drank three cups of coffee from his Keurig. He wished he hadn't planned the breakfast meeting with Harpreet this morning at Camino's. But, he didn't want to jeopardize their friendship, so he'd meet her and hope she would talk about something besides Juliette.

Harpreet was waiting on him and had already ordered a non-fat latte when he arrived. Fortunately for him, she was excited about her work. She was up for promotion to a full tenured job at Salem College and couldn't wait to explain it all to him. He was happy to listen, smile and think of long-lost blonde thoughts.

Juliette also had a busy Saturday planned. She was hoping to finish painting the gallery today and start hanging new pieces of art from the walls. As was her old habit, she'd walk down the block to Camino's, get a pastry and a hot cup of coffee and bring it back to the gallery. It was a beautiful, but cool and windy day. She bundled up, wrapped a scarf around her neck, put on a toboggan and started down the street. She walked past Hutch & Harris, past the Boar's Inn, past Gold's Gym and Mellow Mushroom when she stopped dead in her tracks.

Abhinandan was sitting at a table outside, in front of Camino's, with a woman. Not just any woman—a beautiful woman. And they were laughing and sitting close together and she had her hand on his arm as she spoke. She stepped into the doorway of Mellow Mushroom and looked through the corner glass. It was not a mistake. It was definitely Abhinandan, and he was definitely having a personal and very friendly conversation with a beautiful woman. She could not believe this was happening. Somehow, she expected he would be waiting for her, like in a fairy tale. Now, her fairy tale had turned into a nightmare. She pulled her collar up, turned around, made it back to the gallery, locked the door and began crying. And continued crying.

After Harpreet finished her latte, she went on her daily run, leaving him to ponder his situation and what he should do. There was no use postponing things he reasoned, he would go to the gallery this morning, see if it was open and talk with Juliette. If not, he would go to her house and visit her there. He couldn't wait any longer.

When he arrived at the gallery, the door was locked but there were lights on inside. He knocked and waited. Nothing. He knocked again and saw movement in the back. Then, his heart either skipped several beats, or stopped altogether as he saw Juliette walk from the back room . It looked as though she'd been crying, he wasn't sure. He wasn't even sure she was real. Certainly no earthly creature could be this beautiful, it must be a vision. But no, it was indeed her.

 She walked towards him, drying her eyes as she unlocked the door. He walked in and they stood face-to-face, silent, both unable to speak. Finally, after several moments, he asked, "Are you okay?"

She answered, "Yes, I just hit my finger with the hammer, I'm fine Abhinandan. It's good to see you again."

When she pronounced his name, his collective memory of the English language abandoned him. He could do nothing but stare into those eyes and melt inside. After several more moments, or minutes, or hours (he was unsure) she said, "Are you okay Abhinandan?"

 For the life of him, he couldn't make his brain function intelligently. He blurted out, "I thought you were married." This totally shocked Juliette. Why would he think she was married? He was the one who was obviously involved with someone, the beautiful woman she'd just seen him with. She did not want him to think the obvious, that she'd come back to Winton-Salem for him. So she quickly said, "No, not yet, we're planning on a spring wedding."

"Planning a spring wedding?? What? No! No, no, no….this can't be." This was all his mind could digest at the time. He was still incapable of speaking.

269

She finally broke the silence and asked, "Did you want something Abhinandan? Is there anything I can do for you?"

"Yes," he thought, "you can get a stake and drive it through my heart! Kill me now and put me out of my misery."

Instead, he said, "No, I just wanted to welcome you back and wish you good luck with the wedding. I'll be leaving now." He once more looked into those eyes and felt the life blood draining out of himself. As he turned to leave it took all of Juliette's will power not to scream, "I love you Abhinandan! Please! I love you!"

Instead, all she could do was smile and utter, "Goodbye." He walked down the street in a total fog, unable to comprehend what he'd just heard. She locked the door, the smile that was on her face disappeared. It had been replaced by a sadness even greater than the essence of her smile. She returned to the back room and continued to cry…and cry…and cry.

He didn't know what to do. He called Desmond. Why? He didn't know, he just called him. There was no answer. He read an email message from his grandfather,

"DISCIPLINE IS CHOOSING BETWEEN WHAT YOU WANT NOW AND WHAT YOU WANT MOST."

For the first time in his life, he didn't care what the message said, or what it meant. He just didn't care. He couldn't sit at home any longer. He got in his car and started driving. He knew he was on Interstate-40, but that's all he knew and didn't really care. He drove. He wasn't aware, but he passed by Greensboro, Burlington, Raleigh , Fayetteville and Lumberton before the road ended at the ocean in Wilmington. He bought gas and a soft drink, then started driving north.

He finally tired of driving and ended up in the small town of Nags Head on the Outer Banks. He found an over-priced hotel and checked in. He had nothing with him. No clothes, no computer, no nothing, just a broken heart. His room overlooked the Atlantic Ocean and had a small balcony with a couple of plastic chairs. He sat on the balcony and listened to the sound of crashing waves all night. Sleep was impossible.

He greeted the sun rising out of the ocean with a surly, "What do you want?" He didn't expect an answer. He didn't get one. He stared at the growing light, through the mist, until the sun finally won and he couldn't stare any longer. He wanted coffee. Or, he wanted to walk into the ocean and not come back. He settled on coffee.

He found a small café named Golden Slumbers that had hot coffee and greasy biscuits. He had three cups of coffee and two of the greasiest bacon biscuits he'd ever seen. He didn't taste any of it. He realized again he had nothing with him. Even his cell phone had died and he didn't have the charger with him. No clothes, no computer, no cell phone, no idea what to do, or where to go. A real nowhere man. And his heart was broken.

He stopped to buy gas again and asked an attendant how far he was from Winston-Salem. The pimply-faced kid had no idea, but he thought Greensboro was 5 or 6 hours away, if that helped. So he started driving again. It wasn't any fun driving, it wasn't any fun thinking, it wasn't any fun being alive.

He finally arrived back in Winston-Salem, tired, hungry and exhausted. He had phone messages from his boss, from Mrs. Carter (wondering why he missed church), from Annie (wondering why he disappointed Mrs. Carter by missing church), from Harpreet (wondering why he missed church) and from Desmond, who was grumpily returning his message. But none from Juliette. He deleted them all and went to bed.

His phone rang repeatedly the next morning. He had to return the calls, even though he didn't feel like talking. First, Mrs. Carter.

"Abhinandan, are you alright? You weren't at church. Are you sick?"

"No ma'am, I'm only sleeping. I'm fine, thanks for asking."

There was a slight pause and she said, "It's the blonde isn't it?"

"What? What do you mean 'the blonde'?"

"You know what I mean Abhinandan. Harpreet told me you're in love with a blonde woman that's driving you crazy."

"No, Mrs. Carter. I'm not in love with a blonde woman (he lied) and Harpreet needs to mind her own business!"

"Well, we're worried about you. Come to dinner tonight and I'll have Annie fix something special."

"I appreciate the offer but I've got a lot of things I need to tie up here at work."

"That wasn't a question son. It was an order. Be here at 7:00 tonight. And trust me, everything will be okay."

He next called Harpreet but she was in a meeting. Probably a good thing she was because he might've said something he regretted if she'd answered.

He called Desmond and amazingly, he answered. "What's up Kemosabe?"

"I thought you said she wasn't married!"

"She's not married, I already told you that."

"Well, she's engaged and going to get married this spring!"

"How do you know that Tonto?"

"Because she told me face-to-face. She's getting married this spring!"

"Hmm, I'm sorry to hear that. She's one fine looking lady. Don't get so upset Yogi, there's other blondes out there. You'll find one."

"I don't want….oh, forget it. Goodbye."

The phone calls did not make him feel better. And why in the world did Harpreet tell Mrs. Carter about Juliette?

Chapter 49

HE REALLY DIDN'T FEEL LIKE GOING to Mrs. Carter's for dinner. He didn't feel like doing anything. But he'd go. He remembered the email from his grandfather he'd read this morning,

"THE PRESENT MOMENT IS ALL YOU'LL EVER HAVE."

At first, this message seemed a little too transcendental for him. But the more he repeated it, the more sense it made to him.

He drove up to Mrs. Carter's house and noticed Annie's car and Harpreet's car were both in the driveway. He started to turn around, but knew he couldn't. Incredibly, the evening's conversations never mentioned Juliette. It was as though they made a conscious effort NOT to mention her, or any other reference to dating or women. As soon as dessert was finished, Annie and her son had to leave, it was a school night.

He asked Mrs. Carter how Annie was working out, even though he already knew they loved each other. "Well," Mrs. Carter said, "she's a Baptist. I can work with that. If she'd been a Methodist, we'd really have a problem." Before he could respond, she smiled that crooked little grin of hers. He and Harpreet discussed her job promotion at Salem and they all complained about the weather. It was painfully obvious to all that anything blonde was distinctly off limits, which enabled the evening to go very well. As he was walking off the front porch Mrs. Carter called to him and said, "Abhinandan, don't let yesterday use up too much of today."

The rest of the week was tedious and tiresome. It was impossible for him to forget the unforgettable. He had dinner once with Harpreet at The Salem Tavern. He went to Hanes Park one afternoon and hit tennis balls until he almost broke a sweat. And, one evening he had a couple of beers at Finnegan's Wake, where even the appearance of two tables of coeds from Wake Forest could not shake the doldrums he was experiencing.

He was lonely, sad, discouraged and depressed. That's the only reason he could fathom for why he called Robyn Warren Saturday morning. He picked her up and they visited Weathervane Winery in Davidson County for a tasting of their fruit wines. Then they went down the road to Childress Winery for the opening of their new Muscadine wines. By the fourth tasting he was quite aware he was in no condition to be driving. Robyn was in no condition to be walking.

Fortunately, there was a hotel next to the winery and he secured a room for the night. Robyn looked spectacular. She had on a short dress, with a low cut cleavage that distracted every male in two wineries and half of Georgia. She was dressed for sex and raring to go. He started wondering what he'd gotten himself into…but it was too late now.

They stumbled up to the room on the second floor, had another glass of White Muscadine wine and she excused herself to slip into the bathroom for a moment. Fifteen minutes later she was still in the bathroom and he was getting a little concerned. He knocked on the door. No answer. It wasn't locked, so he turned the handle, opened the door and she was sitting on the toilet with her panties down around her ankles—snoring and sound asleep.

He somehow got her to the bed, covered her up and left her snoring in completely unconscious bliss. He went downstairs to the desk, got himself a room on the first floor and went to bed quite alone and very relieved.

All the way home the following morning, Robyn promised she would "make it up" to him soon, saying, "Abbey, you've really got a hold on me." He tried his best to be as non-committal as possible as he dropped her off. In her driveway, she tried to undress him in the car. It took all his strength and composure to fight her off while insisting he had an urgent appointment at church that morning. He finally got her out of his car and promised himself that no matter how lonely he ever got, he would NEVER call her again.

Mrs. Carter was waiting on him in her seat at church. Even though his head was throbbing, he sang "What A Friend We Have In Jesus" with Mrs. Carter and then waited for her to fall asleep on his shoulder when the sermon started. She did. Harpreet met them after the service and invited him to lunch, but his head was about to burst, so he begged off. She smiled and said, "Okay, I'll see you later." But there was something about her demeanor that struck him as odd. However, his head was hurting so bad he couldn't dwell on it. He had to go home.

Harpreet did not have to go home. Nor did she have to go to lunch. She had a mission and she was looking forward to it.

Annie Norwood's son loved hot dogs, like most kids do. He especially loved the hot dogs at Skippy's downtown. Annie had taken him down there a few weeks ago to treat him for being so brave on his last doctor's visit. They were sitting inside one Saturday enjoying themselves when she noticed Abbey walk by. She got up to invite him in, but before she could catch him, she saw him knocking on the door to the art gallery next door. The gallery was obviously closed and she wondered why he would be knocking on the door.

She kept watching through the window and finally the door opened and a beautiful blonde-headed woman opened the door and let him in. She told her son to sit there and finish while she walked out the door and peeped in the art gallery window. She saw Abbey and the blonde talking and also saw tears in the blonde woman's eyes. Of course, all this information was then relayed to Mrs. Carter and Harpreet. This was a major coup for them. They now knew who the blonde was that had his heart.

Through her associates and friends at Salem College, Harpreet learned who owned the gallery and what her name was. It wasn't hard, after that, to find out where she lived. Harpreet now had a Sunday afternoon visit to make.

Chapter 50

HARPREET DROVE THROUGH THE ARDMORE COMMUNITY looking for Julia Street, where Juliette's house was. She found a nice, small home with a swing on the front porch and neat yard with several plants and bushes planted. She had no speech planned, but had an agenda and a purpose. She knocked on the door and a beautiful, blonde-haired woman opened the front door looking at her.

Harpreet said, "You don't know me, but I'm a friend of Abbey's and I think we need to talk." Juliette was momentarily stunned. She recognized the woman on her porch as the person Abhinandan was sitting with at Camino's that morning. She recovered quickly and invited Harpreet in, asking her if she would like a cup of coffee. Harpreet declined, choosing instead to get directly to the point of her visit. She said, "I think we have a common friend, however, I'm pretty sure he views us very differently in terms of his friendship. Whereas, I am his friend, I'm pretty sure you are much more than that. Is this correct?"

Juliette wasn't sure how to answer, or even if it was appropriate to answer this line of questioning. Instead of answering, she asked her own question, "Who are you? And, why are you here asking about Abhinandan and especially about my relationship with him?"

Harpreet realized the awkwardness of the situation and tried to ease the moment, "I'm sorry, I should have introduced myself earlier. My name is Harpreet and I'm a friend of Abbey's. In fact, our families have been friends for many years. I teach over at Salem College and live here in Winston-Salem. Trust me, I'm your friend as well. I only want what's best for Abbey and for you."

Juliette said, "I saw you and Abhinandan at Camino's one morning; you looked like a couple."

"Oh, we meet there sometimes, but we're anything but a couple. We're probably too much alike to ever be a couple anyway. Plus, he could never be a couple with anyone except you. I think you know that, don't you?"

"I know that we had a special bond and friendship, but I was afraid it was lost. My father died and I had to return home for awhile and I thought Abhinandan had forgotten about me. Especially when I returned home and saw him with you that morning."

"Trust me, he hasn't forgotten about you. I don't think he could ever forget about you. You did something to him that no other woman ever has. He can't get over it. But, there's one thing I don't understand; he told me that you were married. Why would he think that?"

"He said the same thing to me. I don't know why he thought that. So, he's not involved with you romantically at all?

"Absolutely not. I'm 100% convinced he's totally captivated by you and completely under the 'blonde spell,' so to speak."

They talked further and became even more at ease with each other. Each woman thinking she had made a new, long-lasting friend. Juliette told Harpreet about Abbey's visit to the gallery and that she told him she was engaged. Harpreet said, "Forget about that. Go to him, tell him how you feel and I guarantee you things will be wonderful. Okay? Do you promise me you'll do that? Do you know where he lives?"

"Yes, I know. I will...I'll do it. Are you sure Harpreet? I mean, are you REALLY sure?"

"Of course I am. I've been seeing him moan and groan and pine away for weeks on end, longing for you. I wish I'd known who you were earlier. You go see him and do it quickly."

After Harpreet left, Juliette felt as if the weight of the world had been lifted off her shoulders. She wouldn't wait one more day, she'd go to Abbey's condo tonight. Harpreet called Mrs. Carter and Annie to tell them her mission was accomplished. She was very proud of herself and for what she'd done for her friend and also her new friend, Juliette.

Abbey was catching up on messages and doing some chores about his home. Today's email from his grandfather had perplexed him and he'd been thinking about it.

"THE MAN WHO THINKS HE KNOWS EVERYTHING WILL EVENTUALLY FIND OUT HE KNOWS NOTHING."

He thought about going to Finnegan's Wake for dinner, but decided to just microwave something and stay in. He was looking through his refrigerator when his doorbell rang. This was odd, the doorman would usually alert him when he had a guest. He looked through the peephole and saw Robyn Warren smiling alluringly back at him. Oh my God!

She obviously knew he was in, so he couldn't ignore her. He opened the door and she flung herself into his arms and said, "I told you I'd repay you for the other night, so here I am. And guess what? I'm not wearing any underwear!"

"Umm, right. I remember that. But this is a very bad time for me Robyn. I was just on the way out the door to a funeral."

"You're going to a funeral in shorts and a tee shirt?"

"I was just getting ready to hop in the shower, the funeral starts in an hour and if I don't hurry I'll be late."

"Who's funeral?"

"A lady from my church that I've become very good friends with, Mrs. Carter." (Mrs. Carter, please forgive me....please!)

Robyn started pouting, then said, "Well, at least I can help you into the shower."

"No, I'm really in a hurry Robyn, we'll get together soon. I promise. I really have to be going."

"Okay, but at least walk me downstairs."

He thought to himself, "Okay, anything to get rid of her."

They went down and he opened the front door for her to leave when she suddenly turned around and flung herself into his arms again and planted a very X-rated, deep kiss on him, while grabbing his crotch. When he finally extricated himself from the lip-lock, he looked over her shoulder directly at Juliette who was standing five feet away with a look of utter despair on her lovely, beautiful face.

Chapter 51

JULIETTE RAN TO HER CAR, IGNORING HIS PLEAS TO STOP. She drove away as he looked on helplessly and hopelessly. Robyn said something to him, but he didn't hear or care what she said. He walked back inside totally ignoring her, feeling absolutely devastated. His neighbor, Duncan Lacey, was walking down the stairs towards him and said, "Hey Abbey, how're ya doing?"

He didn't stop walking and answered, "Dead Duncan! That's how I'm doing." And that's how he felt—-dead.

He quickly threw some clothes on, grabbed his keys and went to his car. He drove first to the art gallery. It was closed with no lights on. He then drove to Juliette's house. Her car wasn't in the driveway. He didn't know where to go or what to do. What does a man do when he feels as though he's lost the most important thing in the world? The only thing that matters to him?

Juliette didn't know what to do either. Her dreams smashed to pieces by some floozy in a short skirt kissing the man she'd hoped to spend the rest of her life with. She felt the love leaking from her body, as though she had just given birth to love itself, and now instead of feeding that love, it was gone. Why did Harpreet mislead her and lie to her about

Abhinandan? How could she have ever expected a man like him to wait on her? He was not only her dream, he was every woman's dream. Now, her dream was shattered. What does she do now? How can she stay here? She can't.

She drove to The School of the Arts and aimlessly walked around campus, one of the few places she felt comfortable. Near dusk, she drove back to her home, quickly packed a small suitcase, called for a taxi and went to the airport in Greensboro. She bought a ticket for Atlanta, where she could then get a connecting flight to San Francisco. Maybe her mother was right, California was her home, not Winston-Salem.

Abbey went to work, shut his door and took no calls, not even from his boss, who knew enough to leave him alone. Calls came from Harpreet (several of them) and from Desmond. He finally called Desmond back. Desmond answered typically, "What?"

"She's gone." Desmond knew who he was talking about. "Do you want me to find her?"

"No," Abbey thought, "I know where she's gone. I'm afraid she won't come back."

"What happened?"

"A misunderstanding happened. A terrible mistake happened. An idiot woman ruined everything."

Desmond thought about this for a moment and asked, "What did this idiot woman do to ruin everything?"

"She kissed me! That's what."

"Was this woman pretty?"

"Yes, she's very pretty."

Desmond thought some more and then asked, "So, a very pretty woman kisses you and that ruins everything? Is that right?"

"She kissed me in front of Juliette."

"Oh. I'm sorry Abhinandan. Didn't you try to explain it to her?"

"She left before I could and now I'm sure she's gone home to California. I'll never see her again."

"Well, you're a fool if you don't. You need to call her or go out there. You'll never find a honey like that again. You know that, right? Right?"

Abbey couldn't answer. Of course he'd thought about calling her and going out there. But how would he explain "the kiss" to Juliette?

"Abhinandan?"

"Yes, I'm here. I just don't know what to say, or what to do. I'm so tired Desmond, thanks for listening to me, I have to go now. Talk to you later." He felt as though his life began with Juliette, and without her, it would surely end.

He hung up before Desmond could respond. He still didn't know what to do. However, he did know Desmond was right about one thing, he'd never find anyone like Juliette ever again.

Later that night, he had to take a call from Harpreet, she was calling every thirty minutes. He explained what happened. She told him of her visit to Juliette and he now understood why she showed up at his condo. She also urged him to call Juliette, or better yet, to simply go out there and straighten out this whole mess. "She loves you Abbey, go to her."

He brooded through the rest of the night. He stared out at Pilot Mountain. It stared back. He was silent. The mountain was silent. No relief in sight. He went to church Sunday and sat next to Mrs. Carter, Annie Norwood and her son. Annie's son leaned over his mother to look at Abbey and said, "Are you going to California?"

Abbey looked at Mrs. Carter, shook his head and closed his eyes, grateful for the opening hymn to begin. During the offering, Mrs. Carter whispered to him, "I've converted them." referring to Annie and her son. He nodded his approval and she continued, "Those Baptists will believe about anything you tell them."

She fell asleep on his shoulder again. Annie paid close attention to the sermon and her son played a video game. He thought. Harpreet met him in the parking lot after the service and he looked at her and asked, "Is there anyone you haven't told?"

"I haven't told Dianna's parents yet, but I'm meeting them for lunch." He started to walk away and she called to him, "Go to her Abbey. Go!"

He decided to go to Hanes Park and hit tennis balls. He hit four and quit. He went to Finnegan's Wake and ordered a Blarney Burger with cheese and bacon, his favorite. But before the food arrived, he put some money on the table and left. He had to go to California. He knew it.

He called his boss at home and told him he needed to take some "personal time" and would be gone a few days. Of course, the time away was granted, the president would do anything to keep him happy. He then called Harpreet to tell her what he was doing and next called Mrs. Carter, who was taking a nap, but Annie answered and would relay the message.

He read the latest email message from his grandfather and finally understood it's meaning explicitly,

"DON'T WORRY ABOUT FAILURES, WORRY ABOUT THE CHANCES YOU MISS WHEN YOU DON'T EVEN TRY."

He drove to Charlotte, which had a non-stop flight to San Francisco that evening. He practiced his speech to Juliette all the way there. He finally realized nothing would work except the truth. Tell her everything. That he loved her from the first moment he saw her and nothing has ever changed. Tell her he not only wants to be everything she wants, but everything she needs as well. He wanted to tell her she was all he had ever hoped and dreamed of. That he would love her forever, until the end of time.

When Juliette arrived home she found her mother highly excited and in the midst of a flurry of activity. She didn't even seem surprised to see Juliette walk in the front door, it was as

though she was expecting her. Her mother hugged her and without asking why she had come home unannounced, said to her, "Jon and I are eloping! We're leaving for Honolulu to get married and you're coming with us! It'll be great! I'm so glad you're here honey. I'll call the airlines now."

Juliette pulled back from her mom's embrace and said, "Who's Jon?"

"He's the most wonderful man in the world honey, we are total soul mates. He's everything I've ever dreamed of in a man."

"I've never heard of him mom. How long have you known him? What does he do? Where does he live?

Her mom stopped momentarily and then said, "The only thing that matters is that we love each other and we're going to get married. You'll love him honey."

"Mom, how long have you known him?"

"He's my soul mate, I feel like I've known him forever."

"Mom! How long?"

"Well, over three weeks now. But we've seen each other nearly every day and he's the most wonderful man in the world."

"Mom, you can't marry someone you barely know. You can't do this. Let's take some time and think about it."

"Juliette, my mind is made up. Jon and I are getting married in Honolulu and we're leaving tonight. I want you to come with us, I really do. But I'm going with or without you." Her mom stood staring at her, waiting.

Juliette finally thought to herself, "Maybe I can talk some sense into her on the flight, or at least get to know whoever this Jon person is and reason with them both." "Okay mom, I'll go."

The flight was to leave San Francisco at 11:00 PM that evening. They both had to hurry and get things together for the trip. They were meeting Jon at the airport. They had a few hours before leaving so they called friends, closed up the house, had a bite to eat (her mother had a few glasses of wine) and called for a taxi to take them to the airport.

Chapter 52

HE RENTED A CAR UPON ARRIVAL IN SAN FRANCISCO and started out for Tiburon to find Juliette. He was of one purpose and one goal and he would not be deterred by any security guards or by Juliette's mother. He would find the woman he loved and he would talk to her and convince her of his feelings. He convinced himself it was better to be positive than to have doubts of the hundreds of things that could go wrong with this plan.

As usual, the traffic in the bay area was horrible, it was hard for him to be patient. He finally made his way over the Golden Gate Bridge and around the peninsula to Tiburon. He remembered most of the drive and his way to the gated community where Juliette's house was. He thought the guard at the gate might be his first obstacle, but all he did was wave him through with no questions.

His heart and mind were racing as he turned the last corner before the house. Now or never. He pulled in the driveway to see Juliette and her mother standing by a taxi as the driver was loading suitcases in the trunk. What to do? He pulled in at an angle in the driveway which prevented the taxi from going around him, blocking the way. Juliette and her mother didn't recognize him yet, but her mother started walking rapidly towards him before he even turned the motor off.

She started screaming at him to move his car out of the way but stopped as he opened the door and got out. Juliette was stunned. Her mother recognized him but didn't know the extent of his relationship with Juliette. Her mother said, "What are you doing here again? Do I need to call the police? You need to move that car and get off my property RIGHT NOW!"

He never heard a word she said. All his attention was focused on the most beautiful creature he'd ever seen in his life. He had never met a woman who inspired him to love like she had, until his every sense is filled with her. He could inhale her, taste her, see his unborn children in her eyes and know that his heart had at last found a home. Juliette still hadn't moved. He started walking towards her unsure what would happen next. Her mother was yelling and screaming something—he didn't hear her. When he got to within arm's length of Juliette she leaped forward into his arms. Their embrace was unbreakable. Even her mother could tell something was happening. She stopped her tirade and turned off her cell phone.

For the first time in his life with Juliette, he wasn't spellbound enough to speak. He told her all he wanted to, and more. He quickly explained the nightmare of Robyn Warren and his understanding of her supposed marriage. He even told her of his visit here before when her mother told him Juliette was getting married. He told her everything. When he finished, she looked into his eyes and simply said, "I love you Abhinandan, I always have."

Her mother started up again and Juliette quickly stopped her. Juliette then took control of the situation and said, "I have promised my mother I'll go to Hawaii with her, she's getting married. We're on our way to the airport. After the ceremony, instead of flying back here, I'll fly to North Carolina if you'll still wait on me."

"Of course, I'd wait forever, you know that."

She and Abbey spent several minutes alone before her mother barged in begging Juliette to get in the car so they wouldn't be late. One last embrace and she left him quite possibly the happiest man in the universe. A couple of days in Hawaii and she'd be back. He moved his car out of the way and they were off. He had just experienced the most wonderful few minutes of his entire life.

He drove back to the airport, where he was prepared to wait for a flight. He had a "stand-by" ticket, which meant a long wait usually. However, apparently, this was his lucky day. He was called almost immediately for a flight stopping in Chicago before landing in Charlotte. The flight went by in a blur for him. He replayed the entire sequence of events in his mind over and over. Finally, he and Juliette would be reunited with no obstacles.

When the flight landed in Charlotte, he started thinking. He didn't really want to go back home and wait a couple of days for Juliette to arrive, he was too excited. He decided to drive to Cherokee, to Harrah's Casino and play some cards. That always calmed him down and would help pass the hours quickly. Then he could drive back to Charlotte and pick up Juliette from the airport when she arrived.

Even though he hadn't slept in a long time, he was too amped up to go to bed, so he went directly to the poker room. No high stakes for him, just the regular room with the average Joes. He really wasn't interested in making money, he just enjoyed playing and didn't want to lose money.

Finally, after several hours, fatigue caught up with. He went to cash in his chips and get a room at the hotel. He was surprised to find that he was up $8,371. He had no idea it was that much, it was simply becoming just too easy for him to win. This would be several weeks' salary for Annie Norwood.

He woke refreshed in the morning, excited by life and anxious for Juliette to come back home. After breakfast, he went to the small gym at the hotel and took a brisk walk on the treadmill, almost to the point of perspiration. Back to his room, he opened his laptop and answered a few emails and read this morning's message from his grandfather,

"DON'T EVER WORRY ABOUT OLD AGE, IT DOESN'T LAST THAT LONG. BE HAPPY INSTEAD."

"I will be happy grandfather, happier than I've ever imagined."

He went back to the poker room and started playing again. Before lunch his total was now over $11,000. He took a short break and took a look in the high stakes room. Wong was not in there, he usually didn't show up until the evening, so he figured he would play some at this table since he was really on a roll.

He did okay, not great. He was more interested in getting correct reads on the other players. He played all afternoon and ended up with about $14,500 in winnings. Now, he had to make a decision. He could take this money, go to Charlotte and wait for Juliette to arrive in a day or two, or stay and continue. He knew if he stayed, he would cross paths with Wong again and his common sense told him not to do that. However, his poker sense and his competitiveness asked him "Why not? He can't beat me."

He cashed out $5,000 of his winnings to keep no matter what happened and decided to play with the rest of it until he lost it, or it was time to go back to Charlotte. A somewhat intelligent plan. After dinner, as expected, Wong made his appearance in the room. When he saw Abbey at the table, he smiled broadly and welcomed his long lost friend back to Cherokee saying, "I hope you brought some luck with you tonight my friend."

Abbey knew he should have kept his mouth shut, but he couldn't. He replied, "I don't need luck as long as you're here my friend."

There were a total of eight players at the table. He and Wong only played one hand when they were each in the hand. They both avoided playing pots with each other. They were content to take the easy money from the other players. This went on for hours. Abbey winning, then Wong winning; but never against each other.

By this time he was certain he had exact reads on Wong. He knew when he had a hand and when he was bluffing. But still, he avoided playing pots with him. No need asking for trouble. During a break, he noticed he'd received a text from Juliette, she would arrive tomorrow evening at 7:00 PM. He went outside to call Harpreet and explain all that had happened. He told her everything, even where he was and when Juliette's plane was arriving. She seemed as excited as he was, it was hard getting her off the phone.

He decided he'd play an hour or two more, then make the drive down to Charlotte and be ready for her arrival tomorrow. After a few inconsequential hands, he was dealt the Ace and King of Hearts. Even though Wong was in this hand, there was no way he could fold the Ace and King. He had to call Wong's bet and remain in the action.

The flop came with two hearts and a spade. All he needed was one more heart dealt on the last two cards to make the nut-flush winning hand. The problem was that Wong had bet big, trying to drive everyone out of the hand. It worked with all the other players, they each folded. Abbey did not.

Another card was dealt and it was not a heart and Wong once again bet big. It would take nearly everything he had to call this bet, but he did. One card left to be dealt. He needed it to be a heart or an Ace to have a chance at winning. It was the three of clubs. He had nothing.

Once again Wong bet big trying to drive him out of the hand. It should have worked. It would've worked with anyone else, anyone except Abbey. The two men stared across the table from each other for at least four minutes. Neither man broke their gaze. However, Abbey noticed something. A small, very insignificant something that told him Wong was bluffing. He knew it in his heart that Wong was bluffing. He was certain.

He called the pit boss over and asked him if his credit was good at this table. Of course it was, they knew him well by now. He looked back over at Wong and said, "I call your bet and raise you another $10,000."

There was already over $25,000 in the pot before he made this last bet. Wong never flinched, nor spoke, just continued to stare at him. He stared back. He hoped he was right. He was praying for Wong to fold. Three more minutes of intense staring and Wong pushed his chair back, threw his cards down on the table and walked away. He was right. Wong was bluffing.

Chapter 53

ENOUGH WAS ENOUGH WAS ENOUGH. He also gathered his winnings and left the table. Part of him was thrilled with the results. Part of him was sorry he'd done it. Even though he was going to be driving to Charlotte soon, he went to the bar to have a drink and calm his nerves. He'd only drink half his Iron Maiden, but he needed that half. He expected to see Wong come by, but he never saw him.

He drank half the Iron Maiden, then remembered he'd forgotten to tip the dealer. He walked back into the poker room and flipped the dealer a $100 chip. He still didn't see Wong anywhere, which he was very happy about. He left the casino and was on his way to the parking lot when he saw two of Wong's men walking towards him from the lot. Uh oh. He knew this was going to be trouble.

The two men stepped in front of him, blocking his way. They stared at him until he finally asked them, "Can I help you?" The smaller of the two large men replied, "It might be very advantageous to your health if you never come back here again. Do you understand?" Abbey nodded his head "Yes." The larger of the two men then said, "If we see you again, our next meeting won't be so pleasant."

They walked back in the casino, he stumbled to his car. He was certain they were not kidding. Apparently, Wong did not like losing and meant to ensure it didn't happen again. He was still a bit shaken, but was able to drive out of the parking lot and find the highway towards Charlotte. Once he got to the four-lane, he'd almost stopped shaking. He stopped at a convenience store, got a Diet Mountain Dew, refueled and left Cherokee forever.

He spent the night at a hotel near the airport in Charlotte. He googled a custom tailor shop in the morning and went to be fitted for a new suit. This always relieved his mind and helped him pass the time until Juliette's arrival. He tried to eat something, but between the scare of last night and excitement of today, he was unable to. Time crawled. He arrived at the airport two full hours before her plane landed.

He didn't have anything but his phone with him, so he checked emails, texted Harpreet and deleted some messages (including three from Robyn Warren). One hour until her arrival. He went to the bathroom twice, drank a cup of stale coffee, then realized he'd better go into the gift shop and buy some toothpaste and brush his teeth. He didn't want Juliette's first impression of him today to be stale coffee breath.

Finally, finally the plane landed. The passengers filed out, one-by-one, all looking haggard, tired, cramped and crumpled after the long cross country flight. Then, the heavens parted, the sun shone and an angel appeared in the concourse. She saw him the

302

moment he saw her. Their eyes never left each other. They embraced as if they were the only two people on earth. They embraced as if there was no earth, as if they were in a dimension all their own.

In a world full of disappointment, disaster, discouragement, misfortune, calamity and failure....love won.

Acknowledgments

A special word of thanks to my editor, Susan Carter-Hope, who kept me from writing too many run-on sentences. And an added word of thanks to my wife for her love, support and mostly for taking care of me. It's not an easy job.

So give it your best

And don't worry about what some may say

Follow your dreams

It's really all that you can do

Give it your best

And remember that life is what you choose

Follow your dreams

And do what you love to do.

- Messina